Also by Chris Woodworth

Double-Click for Trouble
Georgie's Moon
When Ratboy Lived Next Door

Ivy in the Shadows

Chris Woodworth

Ivy in the Shadows

FARRAR STRAUS GIROUX
NEW YORK

Farrar Straus Giroux Books for Young Readers
175 Fifth Avenue, New York 10010

Text copyright © 2013 by Chris Woodworth
Printed in the United States of America
by RR Donnelley & Sons Company, Harrisonburg, Virginia
Designed by Jay Colvin
First edition, 2013
1 3 5 7 9 10 8 6 4 2

mackids.com

Library of Congress Cataloging-in-Publication Data
Woodworth, Chris, 1957–
    Ivy in the shadows / Chris Woodworth. — 1st ed.
        p.   cm.
    Summary: To make ends meet, twelve-year-old Ivy's mother goes to
work as a waitress and takes in a boarder, a strange boy named Caleb
who Ivy is sure is a liar.
    ISBN 978-0-374-33566-3 (hardcover)
    ISBN 978-0-374-33618-9 (e-book)
    [1. Single-parent families—fiction.   2. Family life—Fiction.
3. Friendship—Fiction.   4. Indiana—Fiction.]   I. Title.

PZ7.W8794Iv 2013
[Fic]—dc23

                                                  2012003224

For Cam and Catie

Ivy in the Shadows

1

Some say you get your best education in school. Others say it's through life. I got my best education early on eavesdropping at Mama's feet while she talked to my aunt on the telephone.

She wasn't really my aunt. Not by blood. She'd been Mama's best friend since they were little girls living in the same neighborhood in Temperance, Indiana. Then they grew up. Mama and Aunt Maureen liked to joke that they would have stayed in their hometown if Temperance hadn't practiced what it preached. When I asked Aunt Maureen what that meant, she just said, "Can you say *boring?*"

So Mama got a scholarship and went to a community college across the state in Hickory, and Aunt Maureen got married and moved to Georgia. Even though a good part of the USA was between them, they'd stayed best friends for *eons*, which is a word I learned because my mama always said it when they talked about how long it had been.

"Eon" wasn't the only word I learned the meaning of by listening in. I learned my first cuss words that way, too, but I won't tell you what they were because the best way to get that education I told you about is to act like you're not hearing anything. You just have to be quiet and stay in the shadows. You go and repeat something you weren't supposed to hear, then, buddy, it's all over.

Listening to Mama and Aunt Maureen is how I learned the secret to making angel food cake so light you'd swear it would float away before you could slice it; it's all in the beating—plenty but not too much.

I learned that sheets under 300 thread count weren't worth spit, even though they were a whole lot cheaper. They'd pill and then you'd have to shave them.

I learned the most important thing last year when I was eleven. That's when I heard Mama say that Jack Henry, my stepfather, was having himself a good old time with someone other than my mother. Probably someone with less than 300 thread count sheets, too, if that's what Mama meant by her being cheap.

Mama cried and cried to Aunt Maureen.

"That's what I get for marrying a guitar player who makes his living singing in a bar," she'd sobbed.

It's a good thing Jack Henry wasn't there to hear her. He always said he wasn't just a saloon singer. He was a star on the rise and singing at Harmony Street Blues was just the first step toward fame. He'd get real mad if someone didn't call him by both his first *and* last name. "So people won't forget that talented guy is Jack Henry," he'd say.

Together Mama and Aunt Maureen came up with a plan. First Mama called McDermott's Lock and Key and had new locks put on the doors. Then she took everything Jack Henry owned and threw it out on the lawn with a sign that said "Free." I know because she let me paint it.

When he came home late that night after playing at Harmony Street Blues, he hollered and banged on the door for Mama to let him in. But she just kept up a running monologue of what he was yelling to Aunt Maureen on the telephone as she went from window to window, peeking through the curtains. "I'm staying strong. I'm not letting him in," Mama told her. I knew Jack Henry was toast as long as Aunt Maureen stayed on the line.

He finally gave up, dragging away the few of his possessions that were still left in the yard.

Sixty days later, Mama hauled me and my little half brother, Jack Jr., to divorce court. She pulled me by the hand to stand before the judge and picked up my brother, eyes blinking, thumb deep in his mouth, and plopped him on the judge's desk. When the judge asked her why she wanted the divorce, she said it was bad enough that Jack Henry had been kissing up some other woman but he did it in the shirt she'd bought herself and washed and bleached to keep it snowy white. She said the least he could have done was take that shirt off.

When the judge banged the gavel declaring her a free woman and giving her custody, she settled my brother on her hip, grabbed my hand, pulled us out of that courtroom, and never looked back.

I did, though. I looked back at Jack Henry. He lifted his sad face, his thick dark hair falling over one of his tear-filled eyes, and said, "Bye, Jack Junior." It would have been a moment to thaw the coldest of hearts if I hadn't known that Jack Henry was such a con artist.

He came around home every so often after the divorce, but not what you could call regular. Definitely not the every-other-week visitation schedule the judge declared. He'd never paid much attention to me when he lived with us, but then he didn't tell me what to do or scold me, either. I considered it a fair trade. Now he didn't acknowledge me at all.

You'd think he would have paid more attention to Jack Jr., but I guess Jack Henry wasn't particular whether you were his stepchild or his kid by blood—his parenting skills were the same.

After the divorce, though, he'd come around saying he needed to see his boy. He'd wrestle with Jack Jr. and tousle his hair. But then it was easy to figure out the real reason he came, which was to beg Mama to take him back. She almost caved in a time or two. I could tell because she'd go all soft-eyed while he was there and wouldn't put up much fuss when he hugged her, especially when he'd sigh and say, "Oh, Cass." She looked like she'd almost melt, and I figured she was a goner. He'd whisper something in her ear and she would hold her hand over her mouth and laugh. But then he'd eventually say, "I can't pay all the support this week, baby," and her face would set hard, like stone. He'd leave, promising to make it up the next week.

Mama would immediately get on the horn to Aunt Maureen. The two of them would talk about Jack Henry in a way that made a person almost feel sorry for him. Mama would be in such a state it didn't matter if I just sat there and listened outright without pretending. I learned lots of new words that I probably wasn't supposed to on those days.

I also learned that Mama was a "serial marrier." At least that's what she called herself to Aunt Maureen. I could tell Aunt Maureen was doing her best to talk Mama up but Mama wouldn't have any of it. "You know it's true, Maureen. Between the two of us we've had three husbands and counting! Why we're a regular soap opera!"

I knew Mama had been married to my dad, Travis Greer. She'd left community college because she was "in a family way," which meant she was pregnant with me only she never said it just like that. So my daddy made husband number one, although he took off before I was born. Jack Henry made husband number two. Aunt Maureen was married to Uncle Sonny, an over-the-road truck driver with a big tummy and the warmest hugs I ever got from anybody. That made three husbands. I wondered what the "and counting" meant.

The last time we saw Jack Henry was in July and he didn't seem different from any other time. He tried to sweet-talk Mama again. He gave her some of the support money—not all—with the promise to make it up next time. When his check didn't come the following week, Mama, acting on Aunt Maureen's advice, packed us kids in the car and hightailed it to the trailer court where he'd moved. Sure enough, his trailer was empty and his landlord didn't even know he'd gone until Mama told him.

She dragged us to Harmony Street Blues. It wasn't Saturday, but to make ends meet, Jack Henry worked as a bartender on weeknights. I had to keep Jack Jr. outside. He cried for his daddy, but I explained that the sign said "No Minors Allowed" and that meant us. I cupped my hands to peer through the window, though. I could see the owner shaking his head no to Mama and shrugging his shoulders, which I took to mean that he didn't know any more about Jack Henry's whereabouts than we did.

That day was the last time Mama called my brother Jack Jr. From then on she called him JJ. It's what she put on his registration papers when school started in August, and when Mrs. Wilton, his kindergarten teacher, asked Mama what the initials stood for on the first parents' night, Mama looked her straight in the eye and said, "J." Then she hesitated a good long beat and said, "J."

With Jack Henry running off and not paying child support, a lot of phone calls were going down with Aunt Maureen, and I didn't like them.

"Oh, I don't know, Maureen. I hate ___ children. They've been through so much.'

Well, now, I didn't think we'd beer ___ much. With Jack Henry gone, there was ___ ing. It was that "uproot" part I didn't care for. It sounded like we were weeds you'd pull out of the ground and then toss aside.

"I know you could put us up for a while but you only have the one extra bedroom. And what if I can't find a job right off? You can't take care of us forever," Mama continued.

But even I knew that if Jack Henry wasn't paying any support and Mama wasn't working, we had to get money from somewhere. I tried not to miss any of their calls, seeing as how their plans affected my future, too. I must have missed a few, though, what with Mama not having the money to make as many calls anymore and me never knowing when Aunt Maureen would call her.

Mama said we needed to start going to church again. Mama, Jack Henry, and I had gone to the Hickory Pres- byterian Church when they were first married—until I heard Mama tell Jack Henry that we were going as an upstanding family and that meant she wasn't going back until he could attend without a hangover.

"But, baby! Saturday night is music night! It's not my fault church is the next day," he said.

So we quit going, but I remember drinking Kool-Aid, singing songs, and making a donkey out of Popsicle sticks

ing Little Lambs Sunday school. After that one brief
spell, we became Easter and Christmas goers and that
suited me just fine.

"*Mama,*" I whined. "Do we really have to go?"

"Ivy, we're in a pickle. Anyone with brains can see that.
I've got no husband, no job, and no prospects. Putting in
a little time with the Lord might be the ticket," she said.

"We can do that from home. There're preachers on
TV every Sunday morning," I said.

"Why don't you think about working with me instead
of sassing me, young lady."

I didn't think that making one little suggestion qualified as sassing, but Mama wasn't herself these days and I
decided not to push it.

So we went for three weeks and I was as baffled as the
Presbyterian congregation when, on the third week, Mama
stood up in the middle of Sharing Blessings and Concerns.

"We've been left at God's mercy," she started. I cringed
lower in my seat but Mama pulled me by the arm to
stand and said that we needed a way to earn some money.

"For six years I've been married to Jack Henry and
have been a faithful wife and mother. It's true I don't
have many job skills, but I'm a hard worker all the same.
I'm not asking for charity," she emphasized. "But I am
asking for charity of the heart. If anyone has a job I could
do to earn money and feels the Lord leading them, please
listen to Him and give me a chance."

Then we sat down and I just wanted to keep going

down until I was swallowed up by the cracks in the hardwood floor where no one could see my absolute mortification.

I had a sinking feeling that this moment wasn't going to go forgotten. In the short time we'd been coming here it was easy to see that once the Hickory Women's Presbyterian Guild took on a mission, things were never the same. Just ask anyone who ever had a stare-down with one of them over trying to take a cookie before the pastor invited the parishioners to refreshments.

After church, the same people we met at the Kroger grocery store who never did more than nod in our direction came hugging on Mama. They told her how courageous she was. I slipped out the door before they could get their arms around me, too.

I ran around the back of the church, where I knew JJ would be. They always took the Little Lambs class outside on nice days, and seeing them now, holding hands and singing kiddie Bible songs, made me wish I was that age again.

"Come on, JJ," I said. "Time to go."

"Okay, bye, Maryann, bye, Adam." And the list went on. I'll have to admit, JJ was a sweet kid. He always had to say goodbye to everyone.

"Bye, Caleb," he said.

"Caleb? What was Caleb doing in Little Lambs?" I asked. Caleb was about my age, too big to be in the Little Lambs class. He had moved to my school last year but we didn't have the same classes so I didn't know much about him.

"He's a helper. And he's my friend," JJ said. "He's been around the world!"

"Around the world?" JJ was only five. I figured he'd gotten part of it wrong. But I glanced back at Caleb. He was a squirrelly-looking kid. He wore glasses and had the kind of brown hair that is the most boring color on the planet. The way he looked and the fact that he made stuff up about being a world traveler made me decide he must be a loser so I kept my mouth shut. I felt almost pious for choosing not to make fun of the less fortunate.

When JJ and I got too hot outside and tired of waiting on Mama, we went back into the cool church. The crowd around Mama had thinned to just Pastor Harold and a man and woman who had given a mind-numbing talk on their summer mission trip to Minnesota, which sounded like an excuse to get in a vacation, if you ask me.

"Oh, Ivy, JJ, come here!" Mama said. "See? These are my children," she told the couple as she took a tissue from her purse and wiped the sweat from JJ's face.

"Kids, this is Mr. and Mrs. Bennett." She looked nearly ready to explode with happiness.

"Ivy is the same age as Caleb. You might have seen her at school last year. I'm sure they'll be the best of friends."

Best of friends? "Mama!"

"Ivy, take your brother and wait outside," Mama said, still in that chirpy voice but looking at me out of the corner of her eye like I'd better not ruin whatever she was up to.

I sighed a great big one, figuring you can't get into trouble for breathing, can you? But I did it loud enough so she'd know I didn't want to be best of friends with anyone but my best friend, Ellen. Then I grabbed JJ's hand and left the building.

When Mama came out, we piled into our car. "Roll the windows down," she said. "I read you can save gas by not running the air conditioner."

"Mama, it's 150 degrees outside!"

"Must you argue with me every step of the way, Ivy? Be glad we have a car." She used her elbows to steer as she put the back of her brown hair up with a bobby pin. "If it comes between the house and the car, we'll be hoofing it."

She'd made that threat before. I had heard her tell Aunt Maureen, "They say to do without food but don't move out of your house. Once you do, you'll be homeless."

"Listen, kids, I have some great news. Two bits of news, actually. Turns out our landlord's wife, Mrs. Morgan, goes to our church. How's that for luck?" She glanced at JJ in the rearview mirror. Then she looked both ways before turning her bright face on me for a second.

"What's lucky about that?" I asked. Last I knew, Mr. Morgan had called and demanded the rent.

She turned back to the road. "She's going to ask her husband to cut our rent in half for the next six months. Half!"

"Can you pay half?" I asked.

"Well, not yet. But I'm working on that." Her face lost its spark as she concentrated on the road.

"Which brings me to my next piece of good news," she said. "Mr. Bennett moved to town last year to fill in as the high school science teacher but a vice-principal position is opening up at a school in Bloomington, near their daughter and her family. Mr. and Mrs. Bennett plan to stay with their daughter while they look for a house there but that's nearly three hours from here. Since her house is really small and Caleb just got settled at school here last year, they thought it would be best all around if they could wait and move Caleb once they buy a new home, hopefully in a month or so. And here we've got that big old half-empty house . . ."

Mama's voice caught. I knew why. I remembered when we moved into the house. "It's perfect, Cass," Jack Henry had said. "Harmony Street. It's on the same side of the road as Harmony Street Blues. I'll never get lost coming home from work."

"I don't know . . ." Mama had said.

"We can get a dog," Jack Henry had said.

Mama had laughed. She sounded more like a kid than a woman. "You know how much I love animals."

"Of course I do, Cass."

"But it's so *big*!" Mama had said.

He'd swung her around. "Sure, it might seem that way now with only Ivy, but you just wait. We'll have a dozen kids and then you'll be telling me you think it's too small!"

But Jack Henry suddenly developed an allergy to animals, or so he'd said. And JJ was the only baby he had ended up wanting.

"So." Mama's voice broke into my thoughts. "They'd like to pay me to let him stay with us for a few weeks."

"Caleb?" I asked. She nodded.

"Caleb Bennett, a kid we don't even know, is going to *live* with us? Mama, what were you thinking?"

"I was thinking about keeping a roof over our heads and food in our stomachs, Ivy. These are hard times for us, changing times. We're in flux, you know."

I had heard Mama use that word with Aunt Maureen. It meant just what she was saying—nothing would be the same again.

"Even when Jack Henry was here, we thought about converting some of the rooms to take in boarders. I'll admit, I'm not comfortable with that idea now that it's just . . . us. With no man in the house." She cleared her throat and a sad look stole over her face. "But Caleb's a child. I think it'll be just fine."

JJ strained against the harness of his booster seat to pat her back.

"I think it's great!" JJ said. "Caleb's my friend. Can he sleep in my room?"

"It is not great, JJ. You're just a little kid. You don't understand," I said.

"I do, too, Ivy, and you're just being mean. It'll be nice having a big brother instead of just a dumb sister!"

I knew I'd gone too far because JJ never had a bad word to say about anyone, especially me. But I didn't care. It wasn't Caleb, exactly. I didn't even know him. It's just that our lives felt like a box that had been picked up and turned upside down. You don't have to be an expert on gravity to know that when things are flipped over, something's bound to break.

2

"Push, kids!" Mama said.

JJ tried but he wasn't much help in bringing the old mattress up from the basement. Mama pulled from above, which meant all its weight was on me. We'd made it to the top of the basement steps and now we had to get it upstairs to the spare bedroom that, until now, we hadn't used. Mama was getting it ready for Caleb.

"I said push!"

I turned around so my back was against the mattress and used my body to give it a heave. Finally we were making headway. When we got to the top of the stairs, all three of us fell flat on the mattress, out of breath.

"Please, Mama. Please move Caleb's bed into my room," JJ said for the hundredth time.

"Honey, there's no room in there for another bed. Besides, I'm sure Caleb will want some privacy."

"Not to mention we barely know him," I mumbled, but Mama heard.

"I'm not saying it's a perfect situation, Ivy," she said. "And I didn't know you'd got yourself a job bringing in enough money to keep us. Why, if I'd known that, I wouldn't have begged for help in front of half the town at church."

She was using her most sarcastic tone. That tone gets me sent to my room when I use it.

"You know I don't have a job, Mama. That's not funny."

"Neither is starving. Now stop finding fault and help me get this mattress into the spare room."

We had always closed off this room. "One less room to heat and clean," Mama would say.

We'd dragged the bed frame from the basement earlier. It was Jack Henry's before he married Mama. Now we fit the heavy mattress and box springs onto it. Mama pulled out a sheet from the hall closet. She snapped it into the air before settling it onto the bed. I helped tuck the corners in nicely like she'd taught me.

School had gotten out at noon today for teacher prep. Ellen had invited me over to her house and then shopping, but Mama put me right to work as soon as I got home. I knew I had some making up to do before she'd let me go anywhere.

When we got the bed made and the room dusted, I said, "It looks right nice."

Mama smiled. It was the sign I'd been waiting for.

"May I run over to Ellen's house? I'll be back by supper."

"Sure," she said, one finger to her chin as she surveyed

the room. "Just don't be late for supper. The Bennetts are coming."

I wanted to yell, "If you'd just listen to me, you'd know I said I'd be back by then!" but I bit my lip. All Mama and I did lately was bicker and I didn't want her to keep me from Ellen's.

I hurried out the door, then headed to our car. Last week I'd checked the crack between the seats for money and had found eighty-seven cents, so I tried again today, reaching as far as my hand could go. I felt metal and some grit but didn't come up with any more cash.

Ellen always wanted to walk downtown and shop at the convenience store or CVS. I'd never been one to care about shopping, and Ellen knew I didn't have money these days. Still, I got tired of looking but not spending.

I cut through the backyard and down the alley and went two blocks south to her sunny yellow house. Her mama worked, but there were pretty flowers in the yard, and inside, why the smell of Pine-Sol nearly knocked a person down! My mama didn't have a job but somehow things never looked quite as spick-and-span as they did here. Not even when Jack Henry was around and Mama thought she was happy.

I knocked on the door and caught my reflection in the window. My hair was a mess, so I bent over at the waist causing it all to fall forward, then threw my head back. It was a trick Ellen taught me in the school bathroom because I never carried a comb.

"It's still messy but in a more styled way" was how she put it. Me, I don't care so much. Hair is hair. It gets messed up. But looking good was important to Ellen lately so I made an effort when she was around.

She yanked the door open, put one finger to her lips in the shushing position, then pointed to the cell phone at her ear. I sat at the stool near the kitchen counter and nibbled on the fresh grapes her mama kept in a wooden bowl there. I listened to her "Uh-huhs" and "No ways!" until she finally finished. She clicked off her phone and dropped it into her purse.

"That was Alexa Ray. I couldn't just hang up on her. She's grounded, so I have to take her calls when she can sneak them in."

"What's she grounded for?"

"I can't tell you." Alexa was in our class but neither Ellen nor I were especially close to her.

"Why can't you?"

"I'd be breaking confidentiality," Ellen said.

I tried to make her laugh. "Better than breaking your arm."

Ellen rolled her eyes and pulled her purse strap onto her shoulder. "Ready?"

And this was the one thing that was starting to bother me a lot where Ellen was concerned. Until lately, Ellen and I would have cracked up over someone else saying "I'd be breaking confidentiality." She'd have made a joke of it. Better than the one I'd tried to make about breaking an arm. But even a lame attempt like mine would have made her laugh. Now she seemed above all that. I knew it wouldn't last but it got to me how she acted like she was a teenager instead of the girl who'd swallowed her sister's goldfish on a dare just three short months ago.

"Yeah, I'm ready." I popped one last grape into my mouth and scooted off the stool.

When we got to the door, Ellen dug her lip gloss out of her purse and ran one shiny finger over her lips. She handed the tube to me. I hate the feel of anything on my lips. I won't even use ChapStick in the winter. But I put a tiny bit on my finger and kind of dabbed it on my bottom lip, then wiped the slick stuff onto my jeans. I wished things like glossy lips weren't important to Ellen and she'd turn back into the old Ellen, my best friend since first grade.

She smiled, swung her purse back onto her shoulder, and out the door we went. She talked about school, about how much fun this year was going to be. She said that, even though we'd only been in school three weeks, we were already off to a great start.

"How do you figure that?" I asked. "Last year we were the oldest kids in school. This year we're at the bottom." We were seventh graders in an Indiana town too small to have a middle school. "We're not even that. Freshmen are at the bottom. We're sub-students. For the next two years we'll be targets for every bully in the building."

Ellen laughed. "You're not looking at this from the right point of view."

I raised my eyebrows. "I thought I just said our view was from belowground. Not much to see from there."

"Last year there were no cute boys at all. Just the same ones we've known since preschool. This year we have a whole building full of cute, older boys!"

I looked at her real close and wondered why, all of a sudden, boys mattered to her.

"Ellen, we're twelve. I mean, let's just say for one minute that cute boys were something we were interested in. We're not even teenagers."

"What's that got to do with anything?"

I raised my hands to explain. "Who cares about this stuff? I've got lots more important things to think about. And even if I did care, the point I'm trying to make is that no cute high school boy wants to date a twelve-year-old girl!"

She shrugged one shoulder. Then she nudged me and said, "Look! She's here. I didn't think she'd make it."

Alexa Ray was leaning against the front of the ice cream stand, one foot on a nearby bench. I had to do a double take.

"When did she start wearing makeup?" I asked.

Ellen shrugged again. "She looks great." And I could actually hear Ellen breathing hard, like she was so excited to see Alexa she couldn't control herself. But when we got up to her, Ellen looked just as bored as Alexa.

"Heya," she said.

"Hi," Alexa answered, looking just past us.

"I thought you were grounded," I said.

Ellen shot a look meant to kill me.

"Mom can't stay home all the time," Alexa said. She looked at Ellen. "Did you bring it?"

"Yeah." And despite Ellen acting like it was nothing, I could see her hand tremble as she reached into her purse. She palmed something too flat for me to make out to Alexa, who looked at it, smiled, and handed it back to Ellen.

"Let's go." She started walking away, expecting Ellen to follow her like a puppy. And this is the part that really stung. That's exactly what Ellen did. She just scampered after Alexa, leaving me alone at the ice cream stand. Like we hadn't already made plans.

Ellen was my best friend. She knew more about me than anyone, including my own mother. And she just blew me off like I wasn't even a person she knew. It hurt. I wondered what she'd shown Alexa. She'd never kept secrets from me before.

And you know what made it stink all the more? Remember how I said we'd been standing in front of the ice cream stand? The girl at the counter said, "You know what you want yet?"

"Uh, me? No," I said, because how could I say that I'd just been dumped by my best friend and I didn't even have enough money for a ten-cent cup of ice.

"Then move. You're blocking the customers."

★　★　★

I ran in the back door at exactly the wrong time. If you're me, that is. It was exactly the right time for Mama to go screaming toward the kitchen sink with a smoking pan. She turned the water on, and there was so much steam and noise rising from the pot you'd almost expect a mad genie to come out of it. Instead, Mama was the one who was mad—meaning angry or crazy. You pick.

"Just look at this mess!" she wailed. "I turn my back on it for five minutes and the meat is ruined!"

JJ came in with a fork and poked at the brick-hard black chunk that used to be some kind of beef.

"Can I have it?" he asked.

"No!" Then Mama started bawling her eyes out. "What am I gonna do? I don't have time to get anything new. I was trying to make a good impression on the Bennetts."

But Mama didn't really want an answer from us. She punched in Aunt Maureen's phone number and didn't even say hello, just "What am I gonna do?" and you know the rest.

I reached under the sink for the Palmolive and went about cleaning the pan. This wasn't the first time she'd flubbed up in the kitchen since her divorce.

Pretty soon Mama's wails to Aunt Maureen became sniffles and then she was laughing as she looked through the cupboards, saying what was on each shelf. I wished I could bottle up Aunt Maureen and give Mama a dose of her every day.

She got off the phone and said, "Okay, this is doable."

She cranked open a can of Campbell's Cream of Mushroom soup and poured it in a pan.

"*That's* what you're gonna serve company?"

Mama tasted it and made a face. "No. Not like it is. But we'll fix that."

She pulled a chunk of hamburger out of the freezer and threw it into the microwave. She spun her spice rack around on its pedestal and pulled out bottles, sprinkling dried flakes onto the soup and stirring them in. It reminded me of when she and Jack Henry were first married and how happy she'd been trying new recipes for him. I didn't miss him, but I missed the way Mama used to be. For a minute the disappointment of how things were made me hurt so much I had to look away.

Mama pulled me back to the present, though. "Tear that lettuce. Make sure the pieces are nice and small. No one wants to put a lettuce leaf as big as a fist into their mouth."

So we worked like that, side by side, until close to six o'clock. Mama dragged JJ into the bathroom. She made him wash his hands and face as well as comb his hair. Then she ran up to change clothes. I must have been presentable because she looked at me from feet to head but all she said was, "You got that table set yet?"

Then we sat in the living room. JJ and I were afraid to move because Mama had that "You muss up your hair and I'll cut off your head" look on her face. It was the first time I'd had a chance to think since this afternoon.

I thought about how it felt when Ellen had walked away from me with Alexa and it made my eyes burn. I would not cry, I told myself. I mean, come on! Maybe Ellen had said she had to meet Alexa and my mind had been somewhere else and I didn't hear her.

To keep myself from thinking about it, I tried to envision eating with the Bennetts tonight. What would they think of Mama's soup concoction? Maybe it would be bad enough that Caleb wouldn't want to stay here. Would they bring Caleb with them or were they coming to work out the details with Mama? I wondered when he'd be moving in. Maybe it wouldn't be for a few weeks. Mama had been applying for jobs. Maybe she'd get one somewhere first. Then she'd have money and wouldn't need to take him in. I started to relax a little because that would solve a lot of problems.

The doorbell rang. Mama stood and nervously smoothed her skirt. Then she pulled open the door with a mile-wide smile on her lips. "Good evening!" she said. I swear, I'd never heard my mother say "good evening" in my life. "Won't you come in?"

She stepped back to let the Bennetts through. Mr. Bennett came in first with a suitcase. Mrs. Bennett followed with two shopping bags and Caleb brought up the rear holding a big box.

Mr. Bennett had kind of a sheepish smile, like he knew Mama wasn't expecting Caleb to stay, yet here he was all the same.

"It was so good of you to have us over," he said. "But we've had an unfortunate change of plans."

"Our daughter was in a car accident today!" Mrs. Bennett said. "We just found out."

"Goodness!" Mama seemed to be at a loss for words. She put her hand on her throat and turned to us.

"It sounds like she's more bruised than anything but she did break her arm. They're keeping her at the hospital overnight," he said.

"She has a baby and a four-year-old," Mrs. Bennett said. "I just have to be there. Not only to make sure that she's all right but to help with the grandchildren. I hope it won't inconvenience you that we brought Caleb earlier than planned."

"Well, what kind of person would I be if I couldn't understand that? Of course you need to be with your daughter! And, as luck would have it, I have Caleb's room all ready for him," Mama said. "I've already made dinner. Can't you stay for just a bite before your journey?"

"Thanks all the same but we need to be going."

"Oh! Well." I felt sorry for Mama when I thought about how hard she had worked on the dinner that Mr. and Mrs. Bennett weren't even going to eat. I'd hate them just a little, if it weren't for their daughter and all. But Mama recovered enough to say, "Ivy, JJ, please show Caleb to his room."

Mr. Bennett handed a shopping bag to JJ and the suitcase to me, which, in my opinion, was a little heavy, but

I was bound and determined not to stagger. If Mama wasn't going to act blown away by their behavior, then I wasn't, either.

"Come on, Caleb!" JJ said. "I'll show you your room!" He ran like a rag doll, the shopping bag slapping against his body as he beat it up the stairs. Caleb followed, carrying the box. Me, I stood there because, as you already know, I wanted to hear what was going on.

"I'm sure it's lovely," Mrs. Bennett said. "But I'd like to see it, too, if you don't mind."

"Oh, by all means!" Mama said.

Mrs. Bennett went upstairs while her husband reached into his pocket and withdrew an envelope. In it he showed Mama a signed paper giving her permission for medical treatment if Caleb got sick. There was also a list of phone numbers to reach him and "the missus." Then he handed Mama an envelope of money with "a little extra for this sudden inconvenience," was how he put it. When he handed her the money, Mama's shoulders went from being all stiff and high around her neck to settling where they belonged.

When Mrs. Bennett and Caleb came back into the room, Mama said, "We'll let you say goodbye to Caleb alone."

She put one arm on my shoulder and one on JJ's to lead us out of the room. But when I looked back, Mrs. Bennett was patting Caleb on the head and Mr. Bennett didn't even touch him.

I understood the whole thing about their daughter needing them now, but I couldn't help wondering how they could just leave their own son. I mean, sure, Caleb was no prize, but I can tell you this, if anyone ever tried to pry me or JJ away from Cass Henry, well, I can only say God help that person.

3

Caleb kept his head bent over the soup. Rising steam made his glasses slide so much he pushed them up on his nose about every third sip. JJ was beside himself with joy to have another guy in the house.

"And when we get done eating, we'll go into my room and I'll show you my LEGOs. I made a dog and a cat and a fish out of LEGOs on account of we don't have real pets."

"LEGO pets don't eat as much as real ones," Caleb said, smiling.

"We want real ones but my daddy is 'lergic." JJ's face scrunched up. "Hey, Mama, since Daddy's not here, why can't we have real pets now?"

Mama fidgeted in her chair. "Well, as Caleb pointed out, real pets need food and care. It's just not in our budget now."

Then she reached across and smoothed JJ's hair from his forehead. "But one of these days we'll have lots."

"Do you have pets, Caleb?" JJ asked.

"No," he said. "But I like them."

"Me, too, Caleb," Mama said. "I'd have a dozen pets if I could. All kinds of creatures. They don't harm you without good reason."

"Unlike some people," Caleb said.

Mama looked at him, her voice softening. "How are you being treated here in Hickory, Caleb?"

"It's a nice town. I feel fortunate to live here. Thank you, ma'am, for the delicious dinner," Caleb said like a big suck-up. Then, "May I be excused?"

"Of course!" Mama said, just the picture of cheerfulness. Caleb put his dirty dishes in the sink, which probably made her day.

JJ set his dishes there, too, like it was something he always did, which left Mama glaring at me until I did the same.

After the boys left the room, Mama scraped the rest of the soup down the garbage disposal. That did a little to lift my spirits because I didn't want to have to eat thrown-together soup as leftovers.

"I think tonight went pretty well," she said when she finished. "Even if it didn't go according to plan."

"I suppose," I mumbled. "Hey, Mama, what did you think of Caleb's folks?"

"I thought they were very nice. I wasn't expecting him to stay tonight, but I knew he would come in a day or two so it wasn't really an inconvenience, just a surprise.

Plus they gave me an extra hundred dollars! They must be very generous people."

"But a little odd, right? I mean, nobody just drops off their kid with strangers like that, do they?"

"Odd? No, I wouldn't say that. They were just in a hurry. Besides, we're not strangers, Ivy! Pastor Harold recommended me."

"But he doesn't know you that well, does he? I mean, we've only gone to church a few Sundays."

"It's a small town. We've been to church there before. Remember just last Easter we went."

"Yeah, but wasn't there a different pastor then?"

Mama frowned. "Yes . . . I guess now that you mention it, he was an older man. Oh, well. The people there have seen us before, is what I'm trying to say. It's not like we've never gone."

"It's just that Caleb, he's . . . a little different." I knew how important it was to Mama that he stay, so I made sure to tread carefully.

"Yes, he is. He's so polite! I wish you had more friends like him."

Great.

"Ivy, you were a big help to me today. You don't have to help with the dishes, too. You run on."

"Really?"

"Really, darlin'."

"Well, okay." I wiped my hands on the dishtowel. I looked at Mama and saw fine lines on the skin beside her eyes, sort of like a spider's legs. Those lines weren't there the last time I really looked at her and it made me feel sad, so I said, "Mama, dinner was good. You really pulled off a miracle."

She laughed a little and said, "Thanks, baby."

I started up the stairs but didn't want to face Caleb yet. I didn't even want to hang out in my own bedroom with him on the same floor. I should have checked to see if the old lock on my door worked. Not that Caleb was dangerous. I mean, as scrawny as he was, I thought I could take him. I just didn't like the idea that he might get up to use the bathroom in the middle of the night and accidentally come into my room.

Then I remembered a time I *had* used my door lock. It was when Ellen and I were ten years old and started a secret club. Just us two. We used it then and it had worked.

I thought of Ellen and sat down on the step as if the wind had been knocked out of me. I decided to call her. I promised myself that I wouldn't mention Alexa and it would be like old times.

I picked up the phone in the upstairs hall and, luckily, heard voices before I punched the numbers.

"Oh, Maureen, you wouldn't laugh if you'd been here. It was so awkward!"

"What was awkward about it?"

"I can't put my finger on it, really. They just seem so odd."

"How much did they pay?"

"Six hundred dollars! Five hundred per month was our agreed-upon price, then another one hundred for bringing him early."

"That should really help."

"You bet!" Mama laughed. "But it's still not enough. It will keep us in food but I've got to get a job. Why won't anyone hire me? I've run out of places to apply."

"No interviews, huh?" Aunt Maureen said.

"Not a one."

"Well, you just go right on back to that church until someone feels sorry enough to hire you. Besides, you'll take good care of Caleb and I'm sure the congregation will want to see that."

"Yes. And it's not torture to go. Pastor Harold's sermons have been a nice surprise. He talks to the entire church but you almost feel like he's just talking to you," Mama said. "So it's not really *that* hard to swallow my pride and keep going until I get a job."

"Our plan's worked so far, Cass. You've had your rent reduced and some money coming in."

I must have gasped. I mean, I heard the gasp but didn't realize it came from my mouth until Mama said, "Wait a minute, Maureen. Kids! Are you on this telephone?"

I gently hung up.

"Ivy! JJ! Answer me!"

I quietly made my way to my bedroom, where there's no phone, so I wouldn't have to answer her.

Mama had flat-out lied to me. She did so think Caleb and his family were odd! And what's more, she wasn't trying to get on God's good side by going to church. She was using those people and making us go with her! My insides hurt so much I slid the rusty lock on my door and went straight to bed.

The next morning was Saturday. I was jolted awake by a loud noise coming from JJ's room. I'd slept so hard drool formed a little puddle on my arm, which was the grossest thing. I wiped it off with the dirty shirt I'd worn last night, threw on some clean clothes, and went storming down the hall.

I could hear the "psshhhoo, pow!" sounds of JJ playing. I ducked just as a plastic rocket missed my head by inches.

"Will you stop!" I yelled. "You're driving me crazy!"

JJ looked at me, his eyes blinking, then said, "Caleb! The monster is loose. Run for your life!" and dived under his blankets. Caleb didn't move, just looked at his feet.

"Don't you two idiots know it's only seven o'clock? Some people want to sleep in on Saturdays," I yelled. I could see JJ moving beneath his covers. Caleb didn't budge, which ticked me off to no end.

"And you!" I yelled at him. "Keep it quiet, would you?"

JJ's head popped out. "No! We're having fun. Just because you can't have fun, Ivy, is no reason the rest of us can't. Besides, Saturdays aren't for sleeping in. They're for dancing 'cause they're music night! That's what Daddy always said."

"Hush up! You'll wake Mama." Which had the desired effect. JJ didn't want to be the one to wake Cass Henry.

Caleb slunk past me and went into his room. I went back into mine, slammed my door, and pulled my blankets over my head.

4

By ten o'clock Mama had a big platter of pancakes in the center of the kitchen table and us all gathered around. JJ's eyes were almost as big as the pancake he stabbed.

"You're sure you slept all right, Caleb?" Mama passed him the platter.

"Yes, ma'am. It's a nice room."

I sighed. He sure was working on winning Mama over and it almost made me sick enough to pass on breakfast. But the pancakes smelled good and it had been so long since anything good-smelling had come from our kitchen that I ended up eating two.

The phone rang and Mama answered it. I carried my plate to the sink and turned to go, thinking that Mama and Aunt Maureen would be on the phone for a good hour, but she put her hand over the receiver and said, "Ivy, wait. It's for you."

I took the phone and said, "Hello?"

Ellen said, "What are you doing this morning, Ivy League?"

Ellen using my nickname was just like old times. "Just going to Ellen Waite," I said. I should explain about our nicknames. There's a sign at Jonsey's Hardware Store that says, "Helen Waite is our manager. If you don't like our service, go to Helen Waite." We were in fourth grade when we asked Jonsey who Helen was because we'd never seen a woman working there. He explained it was a play on words. Instead of "Helen Waite" it could be "H-E-double-toothpicks and wait." We laughed so hard, so I changed it to Ellen Waite. And mine? First time we heard the term "Ivy League schools," we asked our teacher what that meant, and she said, "top-notch." So Ellen decided I was a top-notch friend.

"I've been shopping. Meet me at McDonald's. I can't wait to show you what all I bought."

"Just us?" I tried to keep my voice light.

"Just you, me, and sacks of goodies." In a singsong voice she added, "There might even be something in them for you."

I took a quick shower and didn't even dry my hair. It was such a warm day I figured it would dry on its own, anyway. Then I went to ask Mama if I could go.

"Sure," she said. "Oh, and, Ivy, here. Take this." She handed me two dollars and a quarter.

"Mama . . . no." Don't get me wrong, I really wanted that money, but I knew how broke we were.

She smiled and shoved it into my pocket. "Go on. Take it. You think I don't know how hard it's been on you kids? Go get yourself a Coke and some fries from the dollar menu."

Mama stood there in her bathrobe with a crooked smile and tucked her hair behind her ear, not knowing that the whole back of her head looked like a squirrel's nest. My heart melted a little. I gave her a quick hug and ran out the door.

I waved to Ellen when I saw her in a booth at McDonald's. Relief surged through me that Alexa wasn't around. I went straight to the counter and ordered a Coke and fries. I felt so generous that I put the eight cents change into the Ronald McDonald House container.

"You should have gotten the Happy Meal," Ellen said. "They've got promos for the new Daisy Dog movie."

She tore open the plastic bag to show me the dog that stuck its tongue out when you pushed its ear down. Then she hopped it over to her bag of fries and kept pushing its ear so its tongue licked at her fries. She raised the dog to her ear and said, "What's that, Daisy? You're not hungry? You want Ivy?" She put the dog next to my face and tapped its ear so it licked my face. I cracked up.

"Oh, look! She wants to go home with you." Ellen sat the toy next to me.

"You're crazy," I said.

"Oh, you love me. You know you do," she said.

I rolled my eyes but she was right. I did.

"So!" she said. "I'm changing my bedroom."

"What's wrong with your bedroom? I thought you loved it."

"I did. When I was in my purple phase. But I want something different. Mom said I could so I'm thinking green. Not a chartreuse, not a lime, more neon, I think."

I listened as I ate my fries. Ellen always had a project going. It felt like Ellen was back to normal. Dragging those hot fries through the ketchup, listening to Ellen, well, it was a good day.

"That's about it for me," she said. "What's new at your house?"

I looked up, French fry frozen in midair. I wasn't ready to tell her about Caleb staying with us but I didn't know why. Ellen and I told each other everything. Or, at least, we always had. But remembering how I felt when she'd given something to Alexa yesterday made me freeze up inside. Stalling for time, I took a slurp of pop, which she mistook as an answer.

"So nothing new then?" she said.

"No. Just, you know, regular stuff."

"Well, then let me show you what I bought!"

She opened a bag and pulled out a pair of boots and new jeans that she said she would tuck into the boots. Then she showed me a top that looked like it would have fit her in first grade.

"Remember when I said I had something for you?" She thrust a plastic bag at me.

I wiped my greasy hands on a napkin and reached for it. I had no idea what was inside but I sure wasn't expecting a new outfit. When I saw the blue sweater and jeans, I looked at her and said, "I don't understand."

"What's to understand? They're for you!"

"It's not my birthday," I said. Even if it were, we had a ten-dollar limit on birthday gifts to each other.

She rolled her eyes, then grabbed the bag from me and dumped the clothes onto her lap. "I got the next size from mine so I think they'll fit you." She held up the sweater. "This blue is gonna bring out your eye color. I wish I could have gotten you boots, too, but then we don't want to look *exactly* alike."

She looked at me, smiling. I was so confused I just stared.

She sighed, then said, "Look, Ivy, I know you didn't get new back-to-school clothes this year. And, hey, that's okay! But I had money to spend and I spent some on my best friend, too."

I took a sip of Coke to keep my throat from closing up. "Thanks," I croaked.

"Besides, if you don't take them, you'll hurt my feelings. I'll cry and everyone will stare! It would be your six-year-old birthday party all over again."

She had me there. She'd given me a stuffed clown, when I hated clowns. I gave it back to her because she loved them, and she cried so hard her mom had to take her home. She always reminded me of it when she wanted to get her way and it always worked.

"Well, thank you. I mean, gosh, it was so cool that you thought of me. But my mom, I don't think she'll let me keep them."

"Well don't tell her, silly!"

"Trust me, she'll notice." I thought of my closet at home. I'd never been one to care about clothes and there sure hadn't been anything new added in a while.

Ellen ripped the tags off the sweater and jeans, then pulled off the sticky strip with the size. "Now she won't know they're new. Tell her they were mine and they don't fit me."

Then she set a small bag on the table. "And I got this for me. But I'm going to share with you."

As I picked up the bag, she seemed so excited she actually shivered.

I slowly looked inside and my heart flat-out sank. Makeup. But she said it was for her and she liked that kind of stuff so I tried to sound enthusiastic. "Wow! That's a lot of makeup. You'll have fun wearing that."

Then I scooted the bag ever so slightly so it would be more on her side of the table than on mine.

"I thought maybe we'd wear our new things next week." She dipped her finger into her ketchup and began painting on the table with it.

"Alexa invited us to her party next Friday. We can wear our new clothes then."

"If Alexa invited me to a party, how come I don't know anything about it?"

She grabbed a napkin and began swiping at the mess she'd made. "Well, she invited me and a guest." She looked at me and smiled a little too wide. "You're my guest."

I'd been to Alexa's house before, but not in years. We'd all been in the same grade since we were in Wee Ones preschool. Back then our moms swapped playdates and you thought everyone was your friend. I don't know when all that stopped, when the fact that someone was in your class at school wasn't enough to make them your friend, but I definitely didn't feel any "friend" vibes from Alexa now.

"You know," I said, "I really don't think I want to go."

Ellen sat very still but her eyes grew big with shiny tears. Part of me was trying to figure out how to word what I wanted to say without really putting Alexa down, but the other part of me wondered how Ellen was able to make tears that fast. I'd have had to pinch myself hard to do it and I'm not sure even that would work.

"It's just that—" I shut up because Ellen reached across the table and grabbed both my arms.

"Don't do this to me. You have no idea how much this means to me. Go with me and you'll be giving me my birthday and Christmas gifts all rolled into one."

"Ellen." I tried to pull away and she held on harder. For a skinny girl, she had an amazing grip. "You're hurting me."

"Say you'll come."

"Let go!" I yanked my arms away. Then her eyes sprang a leak. Big tears rolled down her face.

"Since when did you and Alexa start hanging out, anyway?" I said.

"We barely started."

"It's just that, I thought we were best friends." I hated the hurt tone my voice had. "You've never talked about wanting to go to parties and shopping with her until this week."

"You *are* my best friend, Ivy! And going to this party could mean a lot for us. It's so hard to get an invitation to Alexa's party and I got one! Please don't make me go alone, Ivy. Please."

I sat back and sighed. I felt stupid being almost jealous of Alexa. I looked around the place and thought, heck, it's just one night. One stupid night out of my life and it's not like I had anything else to do except go home to a house that got weirder by the day.

"Okay."

"Oh, Ivy Greer, you're the best friend in the whole world!"

I tried to feel good about that but deep down I wondered whether I'd still be her best friend if I'd said no.

When I got home I ran to my bedroom. For the first time I let the feelings that had been tugging at me rise to the top. *Did Ellen think I dressed bad? Was she embarrassed to be seen with me in my regular clothes? What kind of best friend worried about something like that?*

I stuffed the jeans and sweater into my dresser drawer. At the bottom of the bag was the Daisy Dog Happy Meal toy. After I closed the drawer, I set Daisy Dog beside my bed because getting it was the only thing about today that had felt good.

Mama sent us all to bed early that night because we'd be getting up at seven o'clock to get ready for church. JJ groaned. I suppose Caleb was used to going anyway, being a missionary's kid, so no reaction from him. My eyes bored a hole through Mama, just willing her to ask me what was wrong so I could tell her I was onto the real reason she wanted to go to church. But she didn't. She glanced at the look on my face and just got busy wiping her nail polish off. I finally gave up. What good is staring at someone when they don't even notice?

The next morning I was in the world's worst mood. First of all, it had rained that night and the thunder kept me awake, giving me lots of time to think about Alexa's dang party. Now church. I glanced into Caleb's room on my way downstairs and couldn't believe what I saw. His mattress was on the floor! After JJ, Mama, and I had just about killed ourselves to get that mattress onto the bed frame!

Caleb was sitting on the mattress.

"What is wrong with you?" I yelled at him. He jumped.

"What?"

"This mattress! Do you know how hard it was for us to get it up here for you? What kind of idiot takes his bed apart?"

"Ivy!" Mama called. "Get down here this instant."

I stomped down the stairs.

"What's all that yelling about?" she asked.

"Caleb! He put his mattress on the floor!"

"Is that all? Maybe he has a bad back. Now hurry and eat your breakfast."

I followed her into the kitchen. "Don't you think that's a little *odd*, Mama?"

"Well, I don't want to sleep on the floor and maybe you don't, but let's not make a fuss. After all, this is new to him."

"It's new to us, too, having him here, but we're not acting *odd*, are we?"

"Is 'odd' the word of the day, Ivy? You've certainly said it enough."

"I just think *he's* odd. You can't tell me you don't." I wanted her to say he was. She'd said it to Aunt Maureen on the phone but she'd told me he wasn't. That was a lie. I guess I thought if she said it now, it would make the lie a truth and I would feel better.

Instead she said, "What I think is he's quiet and polite. Those certainly aren't odd things. Well, maybe around here they are." She wiggled her eyebrows at me to make me laugh. It usually worked but this time I turned away from her. Mama lying stung more than an eye wiggle could fix.

5

JJ escaped to the Little Lambs Sunday school class with Caleb loping after him.

"Why does he go to Little Lambs?" I asked.

Mama said, "He helps the teacher keep the kids occupied."

"Well!" I brightened, sensing an opportunity to get out of church. "Then I'll be a helper, too." I'd have followed Caleb but Mama grabbed on to me and said, "She's got enough help. You're coming with me." I looked back over my shoulder, jealous as I could be that JJ and Caleb would be having fun and I was stuck indoors.

I sat in church, staring at the back of the head of the old man in front of me. He wore a toupee, which was slightly crooked. I kept wondering if it was going to slide off his head. Looking at that kept me occupied for the five minutes it took for the congregation to sing an off-key hymn. When it was time to "greet your neighbor," I *accidentally* dropped my hymnal and bulletin so I could pretend I was gathering them until everyone settled back into their seats. Then came the dreaded Sharing Blessings and Concerns.

Mama stood. "I just wanted to tell you all how blessed we are to have you in our lives. Caleb has been a joy to welcome into our home."

Oh, brother.

"Thanks to your kindnesses, we now have an income and our rent has been reduced. We feel so fortunate, don't we, Ivy?"

I sat still but Mama slid her pointy-toed shoe over and ground it into the top of my toe. I looked around with a grimace of pain that I hoped they took to be a smile and nodded.

"Now if I can only find a job, we might be able to stay in our home and not have to leave the lovely town and good folks of Hickory."

She sat down and dabbed her eyes.

I spent the rest of worship time playing Hangman with myself using the pencil stub they provide on the backs of the pews. How did I play Hangman with myself? you might ask. Easy. Forget the words and guessing letters part. I just pictured Caleb and drew his stick figure hanging from the rope. I pictured Mama and her pointy-toed shoes and hung her, too. But the biggest one I hung was Jack Henry because, until he left, there wasn't any pretending and stupid every-Sunday-church-going and lying. Well, to be fair, I guess he was lying to Mama, but at least I didn't know about it.

Once they finished the final hymn, a lady wearing about a pound of makeup on her face came over to Mama so I lit out of the building and went to find JJ. I found him outside with the other Little Lambs. The kids sat in a circle while Caleb told them a story. The Sunday school teacher was off to the side on her cell phone. She waved at me but kept talking. I didn't mean to sneak up on them, in fact, I thought I was stomping pretty hard to show the Sunday school teacher what I thought of her being on the phone, but the kids didn't notice me. All eyes were glued to Caleb. So I stopped to listen.

"We tried to set up our tents on the roofs of the buildings but the heat was intense. We could only work a short time before going downstairs to take shelter. We finally stopped until the day cooled. We'd just finished putting together our tent when it began raining. What a panic!" Caleb stood.

"We ran inside. A boy in our group had bought a new tent but hadn't taken it out of the box until we were in Haiti. There were no poles. You can't put up a tent without poles! So he covered his things with the lifeless tent to protect them from the moisture and pulled his mattress into our tent. Now when it rains he brings his mattress into our tent and sleeps on the floor beside us. That's all right. He's a sweet boy and we're happy to have him with us."

The Sunday school teacher finally clicked her phone shut and came over.

"Thank you for that story, Caleb. Kids, let's tidy up. It's time for your moms and dads."

"So what happened next?" JJ asked Caleb.

"What happened first is what I want to know," I said. "That story didn't even make sense. What were you talking about?"

Caleb's glasses had slid down, and he pushed them back on his nose. "It's a story from when my parents were in Haiti."

I heaved a sigh. "It sounds like a *story* all right. Let's get in the car, JJ. Mama will be out soon."

Caleb and JJ turned toward the car. JJ slid his little hand into Caleb's and whispered, "That's why you put your mattress on the floor, wasn't it?"

Before Caleb answered, Mama came out smiling, and I knew the news was good.

"Do you have to go to school to learn to be a waitress, Mama?" JJ asked.

"Oh, no, honey. Goodness. How hard can it be? I'm practically being a waitress right now," she said as she set the bowl on the table.

"Caleb, what would you like to drink?" she asked. "And you, JJ? Ivy? See, I'm already doing it." She poured milk into our glasses. I could have pointed out to her that she hadn't waited for our orders, but I kept my mouth shut.

"Will we get to come and see you waitress?" JJ wiped a milk mustache off his upper lip.

"I don't see why not. My family gets a discount. As long as y'all behave." Mama sat down and spooned mashed potatoes onto her plate.

"But if you're there at mealtimes, you won't be here," JJ said. "Right?"

"Well . . ." Mama shifted in her chair. "Just on the days I work, honey, and I won't be working seven days a week! If you had to work there seven days a week, then Magdalena wouldn't have been at church today, now, would she? And then she wouldn't have offered me a job waitressing at Dining Divinely. So let's just be grateful and eat, shall we?"

JJ slowly took another sip of milk, but I could see the two tiny lines between his eyebrows, the ones he always got when he was worried. I saw them a lot when Mama and Jack Henry used to fight. I'd take JJ outside to play and feel downright victorious when those lines erased and a smile was back on his little face. But I didn't know what to say now. I was grateful Mama had a job but, like JJ, I wondered what that meant for us. She'd always been here and now she would be at work.

I looked at Caleb and he had his eyes closed. It gave me a chance to look over his face, from his bad haircut to his scrawny neck. Suddenly he opened his eyes and whispered, "Amen."

"Oh, Caleb, I didn't even think," Mama said. "You were praying, weren't you?"

"I thanked the Lord for your new job, ma'am," he said.

"Oh! Well, I am just so touched!" Mama said. "And you know what? You're setting a good example for us all. From now on, kids, we'll say grace when we eat. Caleb, your coming here has just been the best gift to us."

His face turned red. Mine probably did, too. I wouldn't be surprised if steam shot out my ears. I'd been with Mama since before I was born and she sometimes made me feel as if I were a *gift* she'd like to return. A weirdo gets dropped on her doorstep and her life is complete. I stabbed at the pork chop on my plate, wishing it were Caleb's head.

When dinner was over, the boys ran upstairs while Mama and I cleaned the kitchen.

"I think JJ's worried about who is going to take care of him, Mama," I said. "I'll be here for him while you're at work."

Mama came over and squeezed my shoulder. "I was going to ask you to look after him, Ivy. You know, it's funny. Jack Henry and I used to hire twelve-year-old babysitters for you when you were little and never thought a thing about it. Now I need to ask you to watch JJ when you're the same age and it just doesn't feel quite right."

"Why? Don't you think I'll do as good a job?"

"It's not that. I think it's guilt that I have to leave my child in charge, but I know you have a good head on your shoulders and I really think you'll do just fine. In fact, Pastor Harold asked me the same thing. What would I do with the three of you? Even he agreed that you and

Caleb are old enough to be here a few hours without me and you're responsible enough to babysit your brother. Like I said, it's just guilt. I never thought I'd have to leave you two to go to work."

"Well, things happen." I didn't know what else to say.

"They sure do," Mama said.

While I washed the dishes, Mama put away leftovers and called Aunt Maureen to tell her about the job. I could only hear Mama's side of the conversation but I still heard a lot.

"Yes, waitressing! . . . Come on, how hard can it be? . . . Yeah, good shoes, definitely. And I can write off my uniforms for taxes."

Then she got to the stuff I lived for, the stuff she'd never tell me.

"At Dining Divinely. Oh, you remember, I've taken you there but it used to be called Ed's Grill . . . Ed Norton . . . You never knew he was married? Oh, girl, do I have a story for you!"

I hurried up and let the soapy water empty down the drain. Waving goodbye to Mama so she'd think she was all alone with Aunt Maureen, I sneaked into the living room and slowly picked up the phone there.

"He made no bones about his gambling. That's why no one would let him near their daughters here! Who wants their girl hitched to a man who squanders all his money? He had no real life at all, just working the Grill and his Tuesday night poker games."

"Sounds like a real catch," Aunt Maureen said in that sarcastic way of hers.

"Oh, Ed wasn't all that bad, really. Anyway, he took his first vacation ever and stayed a week at a casino in Reno, Nevada. He came back broke but with a big old smile and a waitress named Magdalena for a wife."

"She pretty?"

"Oh, fair to middlin'. But she does a lot with what she's got, if you know what I mean. Ed was mighty proud to snag a catch like her. Of course, that was before she changed the name of his business, his gambling ways, and just about everything else about Ed. Folks say there was nothing left for him to do but eat."

"Sounds like she made him into twice the man he used to be."

Mama cackled and Aunt Maureen joined in. I wanted to hear more but didn't want to get into trouble for listening so I hung up while they were being so tickled at themselves.

When I walked past Caleb's room on the way to mine, JJ was sitting on the floor beside Caleb, his light brown head bent over a book next to Caleb's darker one. JJ said, "If it rains tonight, I'll put my mattress on the floor, too." Caleb didn't answer. He just reached around JJ and patted his shoulder.

On Monday morning my eyes flew open before the alarm went off. I must have been really tired because I had fallen asleep the night before with my clothes still on. I grabbed my stuff and ran into the bathroom before the boys woke up. I hadn't had a chance to talk to Mama alone about when she'd start working so I fudged on washing my hair, quickly rinsed off, got dressed, and raced downstairs.

"My! You're up bright and early," I heard Mama say before I walked into the kitchen.

"Yeah, I—" Before I could say more, I caught sight of Caleb sitting at the table.

"Are you sure you only want fruit packed in your lunch, Caleb? Ivy wouldn't be caught dead with nothing but fruit. How about some cheese for protein?"

"Yes, ma'am. That would be nice," he said. "Thank you."

Then she saw me. "Oh, Ivy! I was on my way to make sure you were awake. Is JJ up, too?"

"I don't know," I said.

"Well, go check for me."

"Mama." I looked at Caleb then back at her. "Can I talk to you alone for a minute?"

Caleb jumped up. "I'll check on JJ, Mrs. Henry. And thank you for my lunch."

He slipped right past me. Something about the way he was always slinking here and there reminded me of a snake.

"Mama, we need to talk about this job of yours. When do you start?"

She took a deep breath. I could tell she was nervous. "I

go down today to talk to Ed and Magdalena together. Then I'll know more. Now don't you worry, Ivy. Lots of mothers have jobs. It'll all work out, honey."

"I know that," I said.

She put down her dishtowel and came over to me. "Ah, but these two little worry lines right here tell me that you're not so sure." She reached out and touched between my eyes.

Little worry lines. Like JJ. I never knew. She moved her hand away but I could still feel her warm touch. It almost felt like a magical moment.

Then JJ ran downstairs and slid into his seat, stuffing a piece of toast into his mouth, and Mama said to me, "Hurry and eat your breakfast, now. Your hair looks a fright. Didn't you wash it?"

And just like in the cartoons—poof!—any magical feeling vanished, leaving me with a cold breakfast and the thought of riding the bus to school with Caleb Bennett for all the world to see.

6

I wish Mama would let us walk to school." JJ shrugged out of his bookbag and sat on it at our bus stop.

"It's farther than you think," I said. "You'd get tired."

"Nuh-uh." JJ put his head in his hands, bottom lip sticking out in a pout.

"Don't sulk," I said.

"I'm not!" he whined.

"Why walk when you can take a tap tap?" Caleb said.

JJ lifted his head from his hands. "Tap tap?"

Caleb flopped down beside JJ on the grass. I stayed standing, trying to look bored instead of like I was listening.

"Yes, a tap tap is a Haitian taxi. It's actually a pickup truck. You can crowd around twenty people hip to hip in the back of these trucks. When you want the driver to go or stop, you either shout or bang the side of the truck with your hand. The banging is how the tap tap got its name."

"Why would anyone want to ride in a crowded truck?"

"Because it can be many miles to where you want to go. So you have to decide. Would you rather walk the entire way? Or share a ride with other good people who are traveling?"

JJ looked like he was thinking hard. "Maybe a tap tap wouldn't be so bad."

"And maybe the school bus won't be bad, either?" Caleb asked.

"No." JJ's face split into a smile. "But the bus driver would poop his pants if we all beat on the side of the bus when it pulled into school!"

Then he rolled on the ground, laughing at using the word "poop" like only a five-year-old can.

"JJ, pull yourself together. You can't be laughing about poop on the bus," I warned.

"He's only having fun," Caleb said.

"And you've never ridden on McPherson's bus," I told him. "But then you've never ridden on a 'tap tap' either, have you? Yet you know all about them."

"My parents were missionaries," Caleb said.

"Yeah, I heard their talk at church. Missionaries in Minnesota."

Caleb's face turned red and he looked away. But I didn't want him to look away. I wanted him to fight. I wanted him to give me one good reason to hate him as much as I did.

"So if you want to go around pretending that they've

done something really impressive, that's your business. Just don't go making up lies for my brother."

"Hey!" JJ said, and stopped rolling. "She doesn't mean that, Caleb. She's been grouchy ever since my daddy left."

"*Grouchy?* I've been *grouchy*? JJ, I'm the one that's always there. I'm the one who never complains when you all turn to me for everything. I haven't been grouchy!"

The bus pulled up. I heard the swish-bang of the door opening but I didn't move. I waited for JJ to laugh or hug me or say he misunderstood but both he and Caleb looked at me like they felt sorry for me.

"It's now or never," Mr. McPherson yelled. Caleb put one hand on JJ's shoulder and they moved together like that, climbing up the bus steps.

I followed, not really sure what had happened back there. It felt like one minute I was dressed and the next I was standing outside in my underpants.

All grades rode the same bus and Mr. McPherson's rules were that the younger you were, the closer you sat to the front. JJ had to sit in the second row with the little kids. Since Caleb hadn't ridden McPherson's bus before, I said, "Come on. We're closer to the back." I didn't like being so far from JJ but he was already talking to the boy next to him.

Our stop is the last one so the seats are always pretty full. I slid in next to Lindsay. Lindsay is nice, clean, and her size takes up more than half the bus seat, but she's not what you'd call fat. She's not someone anyone seeks out to be friends with but she's always nice to you when you need a seat or homework assignment. I tried to ignore Caleb but he sat right in front of me so it wasn't easy. I also tried to ignore what JJ had just said to me. I was the only stable one in our family and I knew it.

Lindsay asked, "How do you like seventh grade? Last year was awesome, being the oldest kids in the building. But there's a lot to be said about having a whole building full of new people, don't you think?" I just nodded once in a while so as not to appear rude. I was jolted back to reality when she whispered, "Caleb doesn't usually get on our bus. Did he move into your neighborhood?"

"Uh, yeah, for a little while," I mumbled. We pulled up to the elementary school. That's when I heard it: JJ was tapping on the window. Caleb was doing the same. Tap, tap, tapping on his window. JJ looked at him like he was the best person in the world and I didn't get it. But I loved seeing the smile that lit up JJ's face like it was Christmas morning. And it made me wonder, just a little, if maybe Caleb's storytelling wasn't so bad.

With a quick wave to me and Caleb, JJ got off the bus. Then it pulled to our stop for me to begin another day at Hickory Junior-Senior High School.

I didn't see Ellen until lunch. I walked into the cafeteria and she was waiting in our usual spot, the table beneath the "Save Haiti" banner that told how you could donate your old glasses or shoes to the earthquake victims. I slowed down. The earthquake had been January of last year and the deadline for donations had passed but no one had taken the banner down yet. I'd wondered why Caleb was making up stories about Haiti. He saw this banner every day, too. It must have given him ideas.

Then I noticed Ellen's hand waving like a windshield wiper—left, right, left, right—trying to get my attention. I waved back and hurried next to her.

"Don't run," she said, looking around.

"Huh? I didn't run, I just came over."

"It's just that you want to look cool, you know, happy to see me but not like you're trying to steal third base," she said, and laughed. I didn't. I just looked at her.

"Why the big wave if you didn't want me to hurry over? What's the big deal?"

"No big deal!" she said in a chirpy voice. "I just didn't think you saw me."

Then she bounced on her seat with excitement. "So, did your clothes fit?"

It took me a minute to remember the clothes she'd bought me. "Oh, yeah. Sure," I lied, because I hadn't tried them on. I changed the subject. "Hey, here's a heads-up—there's a pop quiz in math today."

"A pop quiz? Oh, darn!" Ellen obsesses over her grades and I knew it would get her mind off the clothes and party.

"It's not that hard. Not if you've studied." I started to

unroll the top of my lunch bag when Ellen pushed her tray away.

"How can I eat, now? Tell me what you remember." She pulled out a notebook and pen.

So, hungry as I was, I pushed my lunch aside, too. "Let me think." I tried to remember the exact math problems. When I looked up, though, all thoughts of numbers flew out of my head as Caleb caught my eye from across the room and smiled at me. I could feel my own eyes widen. "Please don't let him come here, please don't," I prayed. I might as well have prayed to a Barbie doll for all God was listening because here came Caleb.

I realized just how bad Caleb would look to Ellen with his awful haircut and glasses sliding down his nose. And here he was, my worst nightmare, coming right toward me with a big smile on his face.

I scowled at him and turned completely sideways so that I faced Ellen, hoping he'd get the hint. "I can't remember the problems but they weren't too hard. You're smarter than I am and I don't think I missed any. I think you'll be just fine. Are you going to eat your potato tots?" I was babbling and I knew it, but I so hoped Caleb had gotten the hint and walked away.

Ellen looked up first. Her eyes turned into slits. "What do you want?" she asked him.

Caleb didn't say anything. I forced myself to look toward him. His smile was gone. He sat a lunch sack on the table, then left.

"Gross!" Ellen said. "What was that about?" She flipped both hands out toward the sack the same way you'd shoo a stinky stray dog. "Get that thing out of here!"

I picked up the sack and carried it to the trash can, peeking at it before I did. There was a peanut butter sandwich, a bag of chips, and a juice bottle. In other words, my lunch. That meant I had Caleb's. He was just trying to exchange lunches, and instead he'd left without anything to eat.

Caleb, JJ, and I got off at our bus stop nearly eight hours after we got on. We trudged home, all of us too worn out from school to talk. I took my key out of my bookbag and opened the door.

"Mama?" I called. "We're home."

"She probably figured that out when she heard your voice, Ivy," JJ said. He put his arms straight behind him so that his bookbag slid off his shoulders. He left it where it fell and headed toward the kitchen. Caleb hadn't looked at me since we got on the bus. I didn't know what to say to him so I walked to the stairway.

"Mama!" I called.

"She left a note." JJ carried it along with a stack of cookies and a cup of milk. The note was already milk-stained so I grabbed it before it suffered more damage.

"Dear Kids, Things happened fast. Magdalena and Ed need me today. I'll be off at six and will bring home dinner. Have a snack and do your homework. Love, Mom."

"How far away is six?" JJ asked.

"Not long," I fibbed. Six o'clock seemed forever away, especially if we had to wait that long to eat.

"Come, JJ," Caleb said. "We'll do our homework."

"I'm in kindergarten!" JJ said. "I don't have homework!"

"Isn't this your home?" Caleb asked. "Homework is not just about school. It can be about taking care of your home. I'll do my science and math in your room while you pick up your toys. Then we will both be doing homework."

"Okay," JJ said. "Race you!"

"Don't run with milk!" I yelled, but it was too late. Splashes of white dotted the wooden floor. "That's great. Just great!" I said. I walked into the kitchen and kicked the trash can. It toppled over, spilling wadded paper towels and coffee grounds across the floor.

I grabbed the can and said, "I hate you, I hate you, I hate you," with every item of trash I threw back into it. I wasn't sure who I hated. It felt like I hated the world. When I got the trash picked back up, I grabbed the spray bottle of cleanser and a roll of paper towels from under the sink. I went into the living room to clean up the milk spills but the floor was gleaming. Caleb must have done it.

I squirted the floor, anyway. Because it's *my* job to clean up messes. And because I wanted to squirt Caleb away. Squirt-squirt. "I hate you," I said again, but deep down I knew it wasn't Caleb I hated. Right then, I hated myself.

7

I'm *hungry*, Ivy! Is Mama ever coming home? Can't we call her or something?" JJ whined. Let me tell you, I was really getting tired of the complaining. Not to mention I was starving, too, since I hate fruit so I'd only had cheese for lunch. Now it was 6:20 and still no Mama.

"JJ, let's go outside and play," Caleb said.

"I'm too hungry!"

"Then how about another story?" Caleb said. "This one is a sad one. It's about what it's like to live on the streets of Haiti and not have food at all."

"People in Haiti don't have houses or food?" JJ asked.

"Some don't. There are people everywhere who don't have enough food or shelter. Even here."

JJ's eyes widened. "Like Daddy showed me! Behind Harmony Street Blues. There were people who were hungry. Daddy gave them money."

"Yes, like them. Your mama will be home soon with food for us," Caleb said. "We're lucky."

He had a point. We *were* lucky. There was food in the house, and while I didn't know how to cook very many things, I could cook a little. I decided to make an executive decision (which is what Mama always called any decision she made without asking Jack Henry or anyone else) and fix us all something to eat.

"We're not calling Mama, JJ. I'll cook supper."

"But she said to *wait*. Can't you call her so she can tell us it's okay?"

I don't know if it's all five-year-olds or just JJ, but he was always doing that. Begging me for something and then changing his mind once he got it. And I would have loved to call Mama because I didn't really have a plan for what to cook and I also couldn't figure out why she was late. But I didn't because I knew she needed this job, and if there's one thing I'd learned from Ellen, it was that she'd better be on fire if she called her mom at work.

"I have another story for you," Caleb said. "It's about animals. I'll tell you after dinner if you'll draw a pig and a goat for me."

JJ ran off to find paper and crayons. I went into the kitchen and found six eggs left in the carton. I knew how to scramble eggs. It would get us through until Mama came home. I got out a bowl and whisk.

"Do you need help?" Caleb asked from behind me, and I swear, I jumped a foot off the ground.

"Don't do that!" I yelled. "Don't ever sneak up on me."

"I wanted to help you" was all he said. He didn't say "I'm sorry." Or "I didn't mean to scare you." His responses were starting to annoy me to death.

But then I remembered that he hadn't had any food since breakfast. If I was hungry now, he would be starving.

"Well, I'm scrambling us some eggs. Maybe you can look around and see if there's something that will go with that."

He walked to the bread box, took out a loaf, and began filling the toaster.

Be nice to him, I willed myself. I saw him use the last of the bread so I said as nicely as I could, "Mama keeps a list on the refrigerator. Would you please write 'bread' and 'eggs' on it?"

He picked up a pen, the kind that you have to push the button on the top to get to write. Only, instead of using his finger to push the button down, he turned the pen upside down and rammed it onto the top of his head! Then he proceeded to write as if that's just what a person should do to a pen. I decided the only way I could really be nice to him was by not talking or looking at him. So I didn't.

Once the eggs and toast were ready, I poured milk into glasses. Caleb went to get JJ, who dived into the food. Caleb did, too. Let me tell you, six eggs don't make very much when you're hungry so I let the two of them have them and I filled up on toast.

JJ ran out of the room at top speed but Caleb stayed and put the dishes into the sink. When the phone rang, I grabbed it. "Mama?" I said.

"No, your mama has a much better figure than I do. Just don't tell her I said that. It'll go to her head."

"Aunt Maureen! Hi!" I immediately felt better.

"Hi yourself, Ivy Greer," she said. "I haven't talked to you in forever! How's my favorite girl?"

"Well, not so great." I put my hand over the receiver and said, "Caleb, can you keep JJ busy so I can have some privacy?"

He didn't answer, but he did leave the room.

"What's going on?" Aunt Maureen said, her voice stern like Mama's gets when she's worried about me.

"It's six forty-five and Mama was supposed to be home at six. We haven't heard anything from her. I was afraid to call the restaurant but I'm worried."

"Oh, honey. I know forty-five minutes can sound like a lot when you're young but didn't your mama tell you she got off work at six?"

"Yeah."

"And a restaurant has people coming in for dinner at that time. She probably has to wait until the next shift has things under control, so she wouldn't get home before now. That's why I waited to call."

"But she said she would. She said she'd bring supper." It came out a whine that sounded more like JJ than me and

I hated it. Especially when I finished lamely, "We were hungry."

"Have you eaten anything?"

"Some eggs and toast."

"Good girl. See how resourceful you are? And that will tide you over until your mama comes home, which I predict will be any minute. Now you listen here, you get JJ to take his bath. I know that's hard work. But by the time he's done I just know your mama will be home. And, Ivy?"

"Yes?"

"You can always call me anytime you're scared or don't know what to do. I'm always here so you just call your Aunt Maureen and we'll work things out. You're never alone, you hear?"

"Mm-hm," I mumbled because I was afraid I'd cry with her being so nice to me.

"Okay, sweetheart. You go take care of your brother and I'll be sitting by the phone if you need me."

We said our goodbyes and I screwed up my courage to battle JJ, who is like a cat and thinks water is evil. I wrestled him into the bathtub.

He had just finished and put on his pajamas when the key turned in the lock and Mama walked in carrying a box.

"My goodness! What a night!" she said as she came through the door. "I had no idea waitressing was such hard work!"

But the thing is, she didn't look worn out. She looked really happy.

JJ came barreling past me and threw himself into her, almost knocking her down. "Mama, we were worried! And Ivy wouldn't call you!"

Mama staggered against his weight and laughed. "Oh, I'm sorry, sweetheart. But you shouldn't have worried."

"We were hungry," he said accusingly.

"Hungry, you say? Well, look what I've brought you." She sat the box on the coffee table and handed JJ a Styrofoam container. "We've got meatloaf, fried chicken, and today's special, popcorn shrimp. What would you like, Caleb?"

"Ivy cooked for us, ma'am. I'm fine," he said.

"She did? Why, Ivy, I am so impressed!"

"It was nothing," I said, and looked down. It felt good to impress Mama because it wasn't something I did on a regular basis—if ever. And, as much as I hated to admit it, it was nice of Caleb to say so.

"Well, when I was told I'd get off at six, I thought I'd get to leave, but no. That just means it's an hour after the dinner shift comes on and sometimes it gets too busy to walk out. There could be times when it'll be later, more like seven o'clock."

Seven o'clock. Close to JJ's bedtime. I looked at him but he was engrossed in a drumstick and didn't seem to catch on that he might not see her much after school.

"But it's seven-thirty now," I said.

70

"I know. But I'm new. I'll get the hang of it." She smiled at me. "So, how about this, how about I put these dinners in the refrigerator and then tomorrow night you guys can have them?"

"Okay," I said.

"Is that all right with you, Caleb?" she asked.

"That's fine, ma'am. Thank you."

So Mama put the containers in the refrigerator and then the phone rang. She answered.

"Oh, Maureen! I'm so glad you called. I have so much to tell you! But I just got home and I have to put JJ to bed."

I tapped Mama on the shoulder. She put her hand over the phone and said, "What is it, sweetie?"

"I'll put JJ to bed. You go ahead and talk."

She smiled real big and pulled out a chair. You don't have to be a Mama/Maureen phone-listener like myself to know that meant she was in for a long talk. JJ needed to get to bed. He was *always* cranky in the mornings, even after getting the proper amount of sleep.

I went into the living room, where he and Caleb were.

"Hey, JJ, it's time for bed, buddy," I said.

His face scrunched up. "But Mama just got home! I haven't seen her. She's putting me to bed."

It was going to be a long night.

"She's tired, and besides, she's talking to Aunt Maureen. It'll be late when she gets off the phone."

"Good!" He grabbed the television remote and clicked on a cartoon.

"I'm going to bed now," Caleb said.

"You are?" JJ said. "Caleb, you never go to bed this early. Besides, you promised to tell me about the animals."

"Then maybe you should come with me."

JJ looked uncertain. He looked from the cartoons to Caleb. Caleb shrugged and walked toward the stairs. JJ turned off the TV and ran after him.

And me? I didn't know what to think anymore. Caleb was some sort of pied piper to JJ. I just hoped Mama was right about him and he was a good guy. I hoped he wasn't someone who would hurt my little brother because then I'd have to kill him and I'd hate to be a seventh-grade murderer.

I picked up JJ's Styrofoam container and headed toward the kitchen but stopped outside the door to listen to Mama talking to Aunt Maureen. Her back was to me so I sat outside the doorway but within earshot.

"I hadn't counted on the tips. I got so many! Magdalena said it was because I'm pretty. Can you imagine?" Mama laughed. "Oh, nobody caught my eye. No! I didn't flirt. Magdalena tied this pert bow with my apron strings and set it just so. She said that when I smiled and turned, the men would all be looking at my bow as I walked away and I'd be sure to get a good tip, but I just couldn't do it. I mean, I'm there to make money, sure, but not if I have to pull stunts like that."

I put my head in my hands, glad I hadn't eaten more. I felt queasy thinking about Mama flirting to get money.

I was glad Mama didn't want any part of it but thinking about it still made me nauseous. Sometimes, like now, I wished I'd never started listening in on her conversations with Aunt Maureen.

I picked up JJ's Styrofoam container and put it back where it was. Mama would just think he left it there and she'd probably feel bad that she hadn't put him to bed, which would serve her right. Then I went upstairs to tuck him in.

"Are you sure?" I heard JJ ask Caleb. I leaned against the doorway of his room. JJ was in his bed, covered up, and Caleb was fully clothed, sitting cross-legged on the floor.

"Yes, the animals wander loose everywhere. If you go to the beach, you'll see pigs and goats eating garbage that's strewn about."

"On a beach?"

"Yes."

"But that would be awesome! It would be fun to see all those animals on a beach instead of locked up."

"There are problems with that, though," Caleb said. "Would you really want your yard filled with wild dogs and pigs and goats?"

JJ's face scrunched up, deep in thought. "No . . ."

"It's a bigger problem keeping them out of your hut. Goats have sticks suspended from their necks so they can't get through open doorways."

"Sticks? That's weird. How?"

Caleb picked up JJ's picture and drew on it. "Like this," he said. "And it works."

"How do Haitians know who the goats and pigs belong to if they wander around like that?"

I didn't wait for an answer. "Caleb?" I said. "Can I see you for a minute?"

He stepped out into the hall. "Yes?"

"Look, I know JJ likes your stories. If you've read up on Haiti and you want to tell him about it, that's okay. But just don't lie to him about your mom and dad being missionaries there, okay?"

He looked at me, then said, "I won't lie."

"Whatever," I said. "Just be careful with my little brother."

8

The next night wasn't nearly as bad. No one expected Mama to be there so JJ didn't whine when she wasn't. He and Caleb went to JJ's room to do their homework and I did my homework in mine. I have to admit, it was kind of nice. I closed my door and turned my radio full blast, letting the beat of the songs bounce off the room's walls. Mama would *never* have allowed that if she'd been home. I swear, my homework had never gotten done so fast or so well. In my opinion, Mama could use a lesson in what it's like to be a kid.

Around four-thirty my stomach growled, so I went downstairs to get a glass of milk since it was too early to warm the shrimp and meatloaf dinners. Except when I opened the refrigerator, the Styrofoam containers of food were gone. I forgot all about the milk. Instead I stomped up the stairs yelling, "Caleb! Get down here right now!" knowing full well I sounded just like Mama at her worst, but I was so mad I couldn't help it.

JJ ran out into the hall and slammed on his brakes when he saw me. Caleb's head poked around the door.

"Caleb, no one asked you to warm up the food for dinner. That's my job."

"I haven't even been in the kitchen," he said, pushing his glasses up his nose.

"Then where's the food?" My eyes narrowed into slits. "Don't tell me you ate it."

"I haven't eaten anything since lunch."

I turned to my brother. "JJ? Did you eat the shrimp and meatloaf?"

"Stop being mad about everything, Ivy! Caleb and I didn't eat it. The hungry Haitians did! What's the big deal, anyway? Mama'll just bring more tonight. She said she would."

I turned on Caleb. "Do you see what your stories do, Caleb?" I said. "They make him lie, too."

Then I looked at JJ. "The big deal is I don't want to wait until almost bedtime to eat. I'm hungry now. And Mama told us to eat last night's food tonight."

"She did?" JJ looked confused. "I thought it was just leftover stuff."

"So you did eat it, didn't you?"

"NO!" he yelled. "I told you. It was the hungry Haitians!"

I spun on my heels.

"Where are you going?" he called after me.

"To get something to eat. I can't tell which one of you

is lying but I know *I* haven't eaten tonight! And you!" I pointed to Caleb. "Watch my brother or I'll cut off your head when I get back."

I ran down the stairs, threw open the front door, and ran smack into Pastor Harold. He staggered. I spun around. My arms and legs both pinwheeled as I fell backward. His arms reached out and grabbed me just before I fell.

My heart thudded a hundred beats a second. It felt like that, anyway.

"Whoa!" Pastor Harold said. "Are you all right?"

"Yeah." Then I realized he still had hold of my arms. I stepped away.

"I'm very sorry," he said. "I didn't see you coming through the door."

"It's okay." I shrugged.

"Leave it to me to be party to a major collision the first time I visit your house!" he said. "My mother always said I was so clumsy that, had I been a girl, Grace would have never been my name. Actually, I came to see *your* mother."

"She's not here. She works now. On Sunday at church, some lady . . . I can't remember her name . . . but she gave Mama a job." It was all out of my mouth before I remembered that you never tell anyone your mom isn't home. You always lie and act like she's unavailable. Mama had drilled that into my head since I was old enough to talk, but Pastor Harold had just saved me from falling and that kind of earned him the right to the truth. At least that's what I told myself.

"Oh! From Dining Divinely? What is her name . . ."

"She goes to your church and you don't know?"

"Um, I could counter that your mother works for her and you don't know." I started to puff up but saw his eyes crinkle in the corners.

"She just signs my mama's paycheck," I said. "I'm not responsible for saving her soul."

He laughed hard. Then sobered quickly. "Magdalene. Is that it?"

Then it dawned on me. "Magdalena! You were close."

"Actually I haven't been at Hickory Presbyterian much longer than you've been going. I'm the interim pastor."

"What does that mean?" I asked.

"That I'm here until they find someone to replace me and then I move to another church that's recently lost their pastor."

"They can do that?" I said. "Move you around like that?"

"They can. They have, actually. It's what I do."

I'll admit I sort of forgot about Mama and the food because this was interesting. "So one day they'll bring in a new pastor and you're just out of luck?"

"Yes." He leaned closer and said in a loud whisper, "Or they might just forget to look. Some of them are pretty old and forget where they park their cars Sunday morning."

I smiled. Okay, maybe he wasn't so bad.

"About your mother, I knew she and Magdalena were talking Sunday after service but I didn't know it was about a job. That's wonderful. And I assume your mother is there now?"

"Um, yeah." Suddenly I wished I hadn't been so open, him saving me from falling or not. Because, think about it, I wouldn't have fallen if he hadn't been standing in my way. He even admitted it was his fault. And if the Hickory Presbyterian Church wasn't sure enough about him to keep him, why should I be?

"Well, I have to go." I inched my way back toward the house.

"But weren't you on your way out?"

"What? Oh, yeah." I reached for the knob behind me. "But I changed my mind."

I yanked open the door and slipped in quickly. "Good seein' ya!" I called as I closed the door and locked it.

I peeked through the window curtain. He had a confused look on his face. It was a round face that was easy to read because its normal state was kind of blank. Not blank as in stupid, just no outstanding features, as Mama would have said. He looked kind of young, at least not old, but wore his hair real short so he almost looked bald. You couldn't even really make out what color it was from the stubble. If you wanted a definition for the word "average" you could just point to Pastor Harold and no other words were needed. He did have kind eyes, though. I mean, when you talked to him, you really felt like he was listening and, I guess, that was nice.

Finally he got into his small silver car and pulled away.

I took a deep breath, then opened the front door again. I headed to Dining Divinely to see if Mama could send tonight's supper home early with me.

I took a shortcut to town, down the alley two blocks and then another six blocks on a side street. I came out on Main Street and what did I see but Pastor Harold parallel parking right in front of me. He hopped out of his car and said, "Ivy? Why didn't you tell me you were coming? I could have given you a ride."

"I don't ride with strangers," I said, Mama's training finally kicking in. But I felt kind of bad about it because he really did seem pretty friendly. Especially when he said, "I understand. That's wise of you. There's no way to tell a mean stranger from a friendly one. Although, I'm not exactly a stranger, right?"

He held the door to the restaurant open for me.

I walked by him and said, "No stranger than most, I guess."

He threw back his head and laughed. I felt a kind of smile creep across my face. I didn't really want it to because I was trying to act all confident and grown up but my mouth had a mind of its own.

I hadn't been inside the restaurant since Magdalena had taken over Ed's Grill. Back then it had booths that felt sort of sticky and the smell of grease hung heavy in the air. Now there were fake pink flowers on every table and place mats with silverware wrapped in a paper napkin and tied with a bow. She'd hung heavy maroon curtains pulled back at the windows. It was kind of fancy compared to what it had been when it was Ed's Grill.

Mama had poured coffee into some cups at a table and was on her way back to the counter when she saw me.

"Ivy!" At first she smiled, but then she said in her worried mama's voice, "What's wrong?"

It wasn't until then that I remembered Ellen's mother's rule—that it had better be a full-blown emergency before bothering her at work—and I wondered if I would get into trouble. But then, maybe being hungry with no supper qualified as an emergency. I had to go with that because it's all I had.

Mama pulled out a chair and said, "Where's JJ? Sit down here. Tell me what's going on."

"Okay." My voice squeaked a bit. I squared my shoulders because this was no time to show fear. "Well, it's like this, Mama. I left Caleb watching JJ because I'm really hungry and when I went to warm up the dinners you brought last night, they were gone."

"Gone?" Mama's eyes turned into slits. "What do you mean *gone*?"

I noticed Pastor Harold slide onto a counter stool, well away from us.

"I mean the containers you brought home aren't there now."

"The boys ate them?"

"That's my guess but they say no."

Mama took a deep breath and looked around. "That's just perfect. I'll have to ask Magdalena for more food and she's not here right now. The lunch specials were pretty much eaten up today and we haven't had the dinner rush yet."

"Well, it's not my fault, Mama."

"Did I say it was, Ivy? But it's not my fault, either, now, is it? And I only get to bring home leftovers from lunch."

Mama stood up and that's when she saw Pastor Harold sitting at the counter. She smoothed her apron over her black pants and white top and smiled a real smile, not just what you'd expect from your waitress.

"Why, hello, Pastor Harold! I didn't see you come in. Can I get you some coffee?"

Then she moved closer to him and I couldn't hear a word they said. She was all cheerful, though, pulling the cup off the shelf and filling it, tilting her head to one side and grinning like he was the most important person on earth. I bet she got lots of tips if that's how she treated everyone. It made me wish I had money to pay for my food. Maybe I'd see that side of her once in a while instead of her grumpy one.

I pulled the plastic menu out from behind the napkin dispenser and gave it a good look as I waited. It had paper-clipped index cards announcing the daily special, "Creamed Seasoned Ground Pork à la Biscuit," which was the Trucker's Sausage Biscuit Delight any way you looked at it. The cards were written in slanted, spiky handwriting with little curlicues at the corners. Magdalena's handwriting, I'll bet. Despite Magdalena's touches, I'd guess the food here was just as greasy whether it was called Dining Divinely or Ed's Grill. But I didn't care. I just wanted something to eat.

After Mama brought Pastor Harold a salad I tried to get her attention, but she held up one finger to me, her sign that I was to hush and be patient.

I tore open two sweetener packets that were in a dish by the napkins. I made a little mound of sweetener from the pink packet and one from the yellow. I tried a taste test, which left me positively gagging, wondering how anyone could drink anything flavored with either. Then I tilted my head back and laid the empty yellow packet over my left eye and the pink over my right as an experiment in color and sight. I still don't know which you could see through better because *finally* Mama came over and ripped them off my eyes.

"Ivy, for goodness' sake, act your age!"

"I'm *trying*, Mama. But I've been here for hours!"

"Stop being melodramatic. You've been here twenty minutes. I have customers here and I have to wait until Magdalena comes back to give you your food. Now sit up straight and behave."

I looked around, hoping no one had seen us, but no such luck. Pastor Harold was staring at me. Next thing I knew, he picked up his salad and cup and brought them over.

"Since we're both dining alone, mind if I join you?"

"Well, I'm not exactly what you'd call *dining*," I said.

He sat down, anyway. "Maybe we ought to fix that." He pushed his salad toward me. "I'm a meat and potatoes guy, myself, but a salad always comes with the meal here."

"Rabbit food doesn't appeal to me."

He laughed. "As I said, I don't care for it, either, but I don't want to hurt your mother's feelings by sending it back. Think of it as helping me out by eating it."

The salad had bits of boiled egg and some bacon. My stomach started talking on its own.

"Well, I suppose. If it helps you out and all . . ."

I picked up the fork and shoved lettuce into my mouth.

I looked up and Mama's eyes were huge. She came barging down toward me but Pastor Harold must have seen her coming. If it had been football, you could say he intercepted the ball and headed down the field.

"I should come clean and tell you the real reason I'm here," he said.

Mama's hand went to her throat. Touchdown.

"I'm here on a mission from the Hickory Women's Presbyterian Guild. Truthfully, they're a force to be reckoned with. I'm actually afraid of them." He chuckled.

Well, it was plain he wasn't really *afraid* of them but I knew what he meant. Didn't I mention earlier how forceful they could be?

Mama wasn't playing along, though. She pulled herself

up to her full five foot six inches and said, "If it's about Caleb, I don't know what you've heard but I take good care of that boy."

She was practically quivering and Pastor Harold's nice smile morphed into a look of panic.

"Oh, no! Nothing's been said. Nothing like that at all." He rubbed his hands over his face. "Let me start over. This Saturday they will be cooking chickens and making noodles from scratch for the Chicken and Noodle Luncheon on Sunday. It's their big fund-raiser and they've asked if you'd help. They said to tell you they start at nine in the morning but you'll be out of there by noon. If you want to help, that is. And I'd be happy to come by and get you." He coughed. "You know, to introduce you to the people you don't know and all."

Mama lowered her hand from her throat. "Oh! I see." Her cheeks got a little pink. She pulled out a cloth from her apron pocket and wiped the table. When she finished, her coloring was back to normal. "Actually, let me get back to you on that. I'm the only waitress here right now and I'm a little busy." And, like she'd been shot out of a cannon, she was gone.

Pastor Harold exhaled and slumped in his chair. I continued stuffing my face. I felt sorry for him, though. He wasn't the first person to get a taste of Cass Henry's indignation. I, myself, experienced it on a daily basis.

"It's just her way," I said between mouthfuls.

"Pardon me?"

"Mama." I wiped my mouth on a napkin. "It had nothing to do with you. When she feels like she's being judged, it gets her back up. That's all."

"Oh." He looked relieved. "I meant no harm. Truth is, those women in the Guild are relentless. I can guarantee the first thing they'll ask when one of them sees me is 'Did you talk to Cass Henry about helping out?' "

"They like helping others but they expect something in return," I said.

"Yes! That's it exactly," he said.

And because I knew that Mama had really gotten help from the people at church, she'd probably come around and work the luncheon. Besides, I felt sorry for Pastor Harold so I said, "She'll help. Wait and see."

Then Mama brought over his dinner.

"Thank you!" he said. Maybe a little enthusiastically, but, as I said, I've been where he is now so I understand the power of overcompensating.

Mama set the plate down and refilled his cup with steaming coffee.

"Ivy, Magdalena's in the kitchen now. Come with me. And, Pastor Harold?"

"Yes?" He looked at her.

"I'll come Saturday. And, well . . ." She pulled her hair over to one side and her face took on that pink blush again. "I'd be grateful to take you up on that ride."

Then she went from looking all nice and sweet to

saying in her brisk voice—the one I'm more used to—
"Ivy, come."

I hopped off my chair but looked back as I followed
Mama. Pastor Harold's eyes met mine and I felt like we
were both hanging on, caught up in the wake of Mama.

9

O h, honey, of *course* you can send home food for your babies!" Magdalena said to Mama.

She pulled out three Styrofoam trays and began piling in biscuits with sausage gravy.

"I'm really sorry about this," Mama said. "I'll get to the bottom of what happened to the food when I get home."

"Now don't you worry. Those boys were just hungry. No need to make them feel bad about that." Magdalena flashed a smile at me. "You sure are a pretty thing."

I'd have liked to return the compliment but she had on so much makeup I couldn't really tell if she was pretty or not. Instead I just smiled my thanks. She stacked the containers in my arms and Mama walked me to the door. "Hurry on home, now. And don't spill them!"

"Which do you want me to do? Hurry or not spill them?" I asked. Even through the Styrofoam, I could feel the heat of the gravy. Plus they were heavy and awkward.

"I'll be happy to drive her." Pastor Harold handed Ed some bills at the cash register, then opened the door for me.

"That would be so *sweet* of you!" Mama's voice practically dripped in syrup.

"No problem!" he said.

Did anyone ask me if it was a problem? Or if I wanted to go with him? No, they did not. But I really didn't want to walk all that way, and if Pastor Harold turned out to be a serial killer and this was the end of me, well, that would serve Mama right, wouldn't it?

Pastor Harold opened the rounded trunk of his car and set the containers flat on the floor. There wasn't much room for anything else.

"They'll ride better this way." He slammed the trunk shut.

"Is this the world's smallest car?" I asked. "It's a wonder you fit inside."

"Well, I do have an old beat-up truck that I use sometimes. It's almost as old as I am." He laughed. "But I drive this because I like to think of it as doing my best to conserve fuel—and money, of which I don't have a lot." He smiled that nice smile again.

"I prefer to think of it as a futuristic Easter egg," I said.

He laughed. "Ivy, you're all right."

"I know that." I tossed my head so my hair would swing back but I looked out my side window so he wouldn't see how happy his words made me. "So they must not pay interim preachers a lot, huh?"

"Nope," he said. "But then, they don't pay regular ones much, either. That's why it's referred to as a 'calling.' You have to get your pleasure from helping people, not from your salary."

"Well, if you wanted to both help people and make money, why didn't you let Caleb move in with *you*? You could have helped the Bennetts and got paid, too." Not to mention, I wouldn't be stuck with him.

"Lots of reasons, I guess. I've never been married *or* a father so I thought Caleb would do better with a family. I'd heard enough good things about your mother to feel comfortable recommending her. And it all happened so fast. I didn't know much about the Bennetts so I didn't realize they were looking for a place for him to stay. Their mission talk was scheduled before I came to this church."

He stopped the car, unbuckled his seat belt, and popped the trunk. It took me a minute to think about what he said. When I got to the back of the car, he handed me one of the dinners and said he'd carry the other two.

"Wait." I shifted the container then looked him in the eye. "Do you realize what you just said? You don't know the Bennetts at all yet you let my mother move Caleb into the same house as us." I thought about Caleb's claim that he'd been to Haiti when it was as obvious as the nose on his face that his parents were strictly the Minnesota Missionary types. "I've caught him lying. Now he may be stealing food from us and lying about that as well. Doesn't any of that bother you?"

"Stealing? And lying? What kind of lies?"

"He fills JJ's head with his 'world travels.' Do you think that's true?"

"That Caleb has traveled the world? Not that I know of."

"Then that's a lie." I focused on that instead of how sometimes I let him tell those fibs to keep JJ occupied. Still, lying was lying, right? "Mama said Mr. Bennett was a teacher and now he's a vice principal. And you heard their talk on mission work in Minnesota. You know Mr. and Mrs. Bennett have probably never traveled anywhere that didn't have a Holiday Inn."

His forehead was scrunched like he was thinking. "Lots of people hold down jobs and still do mission work. As for them not traveling for it, maybe Caleb is embarrassed that they haven't. Maybe he's trying to make you—and himself—feel they're doing something important."

"And maybe he's a psycho, but we don't know, do we? Because here we are, stuck with him, and no one but me worries about it at all."

He seemed to be absorbing what I said. Problem is, it took him a little too long and I was way too mad. "You know what?" I said. "I don't need your help getting the food into the house. Thanks for the ride."

I grabbed the Styrofoam containers from him and marched up the sidewalk before he knew what hit him.

"Ivy, wait!" he called. "At least let me get the door."

"You've done enough."

And it was a little bit of a struggle getting the door open but I did it myself. I didn't need his help with the food or anything else. I could handle taking care of my own family.

JJ almost knocked me over as soon as I walked in. He snatched one of the containers out of my hands and darted off with it. He sure didn't act like a kid who had already eaten. I set Caleb's down on the kitchen table—not directly handing it to him—then gave him a look that even an idiot would know meant that I suspected he'd lied to me and had already eaten. I took my own container up to my room to eat alone.

I wasn't even halfway through when the phone rang and it was Ellen.

"Ivy League! Whatcha doin'?"

"Oh, just finishing my dinner."

"When you get done, why don't you bring your new clothes over so I can see you in them?"

"Let me finish this last bite." I swallowed hard. A Trucker's Sausage Biscuit Delight isn't the easiest thing to get down, plus I needed time to think. I'd told Ellen the clothes fit when I didn't know if they did or not.

"I can't come. See, Mama's at work right now and I have to babysit JJ."

"Oh! No problemo. I'll just come over there. See you in ten."

"No! Wait!" But she'd hung up.

"Crap, crap, double crap!" I yanked open my dresser

drawer and pulled out the clothes. One thing I knew was that I didn't want her to see Caleb here.

I quickly pulled the T-shirt I'd been wearing over my head and stepped out of my old jeans. I struggled into the blue sweater. It fit tighter and shorter than I like but it didn't show my stomach once I tugged the jeans on. I was just snapping them when I heard the doorbell.

"I'll get it!" I yelled, racing down the stairs.

I glanced toward the kitchen and saw Caleb looking down the hall at me but he stayed put, thank God. I yanked the door open and stepped outside real quick.

"Hey!" I said.

"Oh! Look how awesome you look! See, I knew that blue was an amazing color for you."

"Yep. Uh-huh. You did a good job picking them out," I said, smoothing the front of the sweater.

"Let's go inside and practice putting on makeup," she said. "I know it's not something you're used to."

"Oh! Well . . ." Good grief, how was I going to get out of this? "Did I mention that JJ is sick?" I crossed my fingers behind my back because Aunt Maureen told me once that if you tell a lie, it might come true.

"No, what's the matter with him?"

"I guess I won't know until Mama gets home later. I don't want you to catch it so I'd hate for you to come in-side."

"No worries. I can put it on you right here. Bring a mirror out so you can learn how to apply it yourself."

I took two deep breaths. Now I not only had to keep her out, I had to keep JJ and Caleb in. Plus I had to wear makeup.

"Wait here."

I ran into the kitchen first. "Caleb?"

He looked up from washing his fork.

"I need you to keep JJ inside and I need you to not ask me why." Dang, I hated asking for help, especially from him, so I ended with "Can you help me or not? 'Cause if you can't, don't say you can."

"I'll read a story to JJ upstairs." Which, I knew from experience, was the closest I was going to get to a "yes."

"Okay." I took the stairs two at a time. I skidded to a halt in my room, then lifted the mirror off my wall since I didn't have anything smaller.

"Ivy, what're you doing?" JJ asked.

"Never mind. Stay put! Caleb will be right up." I ran downstairs.

"Why?"

"He's going to read you a story!" I yelled over my shoulder, and hurried back outside.

I slid down onto the step next to Ellen. "Whew!" I pulled the sweater away from my sweaty neck.

She unscrewed the cap off a tube of cream and squirted some pink-colored stuff out onto her hand. "This is foundation. We'll rub this all over your face."

"Oh, Ellen, maybe this isn't the best time. I mean, I'm sweaty. It's hot. Do we have to do it now?"

She put her foundation-free hand on her hip. "I knew this would happen, Ivy. It's not right for you to be so stubborn when I'm sharing this with you plus giving you a free lesson on how to wear it."

"I appreciate all that, Ellen, really I do." Okay, I didn't but I also didn't want to fight. "But . . . is my face so bad the way it is?"

"I didn't say that. But everyone can use some help. I mean, you've got deep-set eyes, for heaven's sake. That makes them look close together. A little color on the outside corners will separate them more. And some bronzer might make your nose look longer and not so pugged. Not to mention your lips."

"Okay! Okay. I get the idea."

I tilted my head up so she could get to my face but it really stung to hear that she thought my eyes were too close together and I had a pug nose. She made me sound like I had a pig's face.

She'd just finished slathering on the foundation when the door opened with a bang and JJ ran down the porch stairs.

"JJ!" I called.

"He doesn't look sick to me," Ellen said.

"Um . . . symptoms come and go." I hopped up and ran after my little brother. I caught up with him as he was rounding the corner of the house.

"You're supposed to stay inside!" I said.

"I don't wanna! Let go, Ivy!"

Then Caleb came running, too. "I was only in the bathroom for a minute."

Ellen said, "What's he doing here?"

But JJ was putting up a real struggle. I realized it didn't matter if he stayed outside or not since Ellen had seen Caleb, so I let go. When I did, he staggered and clutched his stomach. He turned away from us and out fell brown and creamy chunks.

"Ew! He's vomiting!" Ellen jumped up.

"JJ! Are you all right, buddy?" I felt terrible. I'd lied and said he was sick and now he really was.

"Ivy, you know I can't stand vomit!" Ellen took off running. She was skinny and quick, already almost half a block away.

"I'll call you later!" I yelled after her.

I looked at my little brother. This was my fault. I put my hand on JJ's forehead, like Mama always did, to check for a fever. But that's when I realized that he wasn't clutching his stomach because it hurt.

"That's not vomit, mister. That's your supper." I pulled his hands from his stomach and the crushed Styrofoam container fell with the biscuits spilling from it. "Just where were you going with it?"

"I was just gonna eat outside, that's all!" he said.

"That's a lie, JJ." I looked at Caleb. "Good people don't lie or make up stories. Now get inside this very minute. You need a bath."

"I don't want a bath!"

But I didn't want Mama coming home to find him this way, especially when I'd already bothered her at the restaurant. So I said, "You should have thought before you ran out here and made such a mess."

"But Caleb is reading me a story."

"I'll *tell* you a story instead," Caleb said. "Come. It's a funny story. About bathing."

We all went inside. I ran a bubble bath for JJ. He raised his arms and I pulled his gooey shirt off. It made me feel sad for a minute to see how little he looked without a shirt on. Like he was still a baby.

"Okay, hop in," I said.

He jumped in with a plop, spraying the floor with soap bubbles. He splashed around, sending more bubbles flying. I wondered how Mama got anything done, as much work as this kid was.

"Caleb!" I called. "Wasn't there a story you were gonna tell?"

He came into the room and turned the light out.

"Hey!" I said. "What're you doing?"

"Fluorescent lighting can be very distracting." Caleb sat on the floor. "Natural lighting is more soothing."

"Whatever." There was enough light coming in through the window. I lathered up the washcloth and tried to catch JJ's face.

"Is it a story about Haiti?" JJ pushed my hand away.

"It's about the outdoor shower that was built there to accommodate the missionaries."

JJ stopped squirming, completely focused on Caleb, which gave *me* time to focus—on his dirty neck.

"This new shower didn't smell bad the way the old indoor one did but was much draftier because there was no roof," Caleb said. "I was showering when I first heard laughter. As it kept up, I began looking around and found that the Haitians had knocked a hole in the shower wall and several people were watching me as I bathed."

"They saw you naked?" JJ's voice was high.

"No, luckily I had worn my swimsuit."

I listened because, as I've already told you, that's the best way to find out anything. Anyway, as I listened, it occurred to me that "bathed" and "swimsuit" weren't words a boy our age usually used. Weird.

Caleb continued. "One of the men from the compound came to investigate and stayed in the shower with me to guard the hole. He would spit in the person's face whenever they looked through the hole. After a time, he got tired so I filled my soap dish with water and threw the soapy mixture out the hole whenever a face appeared."

JJ squealed with laughter. "Like this?" And he cupped his hands into the soapy bathwater and threw it at Caleb, getting me wet in the bargain.

"JJ Henry! Look at what you've done!" I said.

JJ jumped from the tub. I tried to grab him but he slipped out of my hands like a wet catfish. He sloshed down the hall, trailing water.

Caleb headed after him.

"*I'll* take care of my brother!" I pushed past him, then slid in a water puddle and fell, banging my shoulder on the doorframe.

"JJ, get back here this instant!" I called, rubbing my sore arm. I sidestepped the trail of water he left and got just past Mama's room when the phone rang. JJ began chanting, "No! I'm running from the nosy people! I'm hiding from those nosy Haitians!"

I grabbed the phone and shouted, "What?!" into the receiver, trying to be heard over JJ's ranting.

There was silence for a beat and then Aunt Maureen's voice said, "I guess I don't need to ask how things are going there. Sounds like the place is going to hell in a handbasket."

What could I say? She was right. And with me in charge, too. That's when I started bawling like a big ole baby.

10

I sat with my legs drawn up under my favorite nightgown, an old flannel one that used to touch the floor.
I liked its softness so much I just kept on wearing it while
my body grew two feet taller. Now it came above my
knees, but wearing it always made me feel safe and, tonight, I needed it. Mama was soaking her feet in the
kitchen and talking to Aunt Maureen. Listening was more
like it. And that meant I wasn't hearing much of the conversation.

Before Mama had come home, Aunt Maureen had
calmed me down. I'd taken off the clothes Ellen had
bought me and showered. Caleb had corralled JJ, dressed
him in pajamas, and read him a story. JJ was asleep before
Mama got here.

But Aunt Maureen had called her right after Mama
arrived. I'm sure Mama heard all about how Aunt Maureen had to get me to stop crying and give me tips on
calming JJ down for the night.

"He's never been wild like this before!" I'd sobbed to her.

"He's always had his mother home at night, Ivy. He's so young. He thinks it's playtime. He needs to know the rules haven't changed."

But they have.

"He needs to know who's boss."

Me, too.

"You've got to be strong for him, Ivy."

Who's going to be strong for me?

And now I figured both she and Mama were talking about what a failure I was. I wished Mama would do more than say "Mm-hm. Yes, I see." It was giving me nothing to go on and I wasn't feeling brave enough to chance her hearing me pick up the phone. Finally I just went to bed because babysitting was turning into a job that completely wore me out.

I got through the next two days all right. JJ didn't seem quite as bad, or maybe I was getting used to it. I'd gone outside to eat at lunchtime to avoid Ellen. I'd been embarrassed to face her after she'd seen Caleb at my house. But on Friday morning, Ellen was waiting. She nabbed me the second I got off the school bus.

"Hey!" she said. "I thought you said you'd call me."

"I did? Sorry."

"I was starting to think you were avoiding me."

"Oh. No," I said. "I've just been busy."

"Too busy to eat lunch?"

"Well, um, JJ was sick and all so I thought I might be contagious" was the best I could come up with.

"So, how's your brother?"

"He's fine now." Which was probably the first true thing I'd said since I got off the bus.

Ellen shook all over as if the memory of seeing JJ "vomit" still had her shuddering.

"That's good. What was that weird kid doing at your house?"

I'd been expecting this question but didn't have a good answer in mind. "Oh, he's new to the neighborhood. Just visiting, I guess."

I picked up speed on the way into the school building because I didn't know if Caleb was behind me.

"Well, anyway, you're going to look so cool tonight! I cannot wait. We'll have so much fun at Alexa's party."

"Uh-huh," I said because, really, nothing in my life was in my control anymore so why should going to that stupid party be, either?

"It starts at six."

"Six!" I said. Mama got home between 6:30 and 7:00. There was no way she would approve of me going to a party like the kind Alexa would have.

"Yes, but we're going earlier. I need to be there at five-thirty."

Five-thirty wouldn't give me much time there. But if Caleb watched JJ, I could go, and maybe Ellen would find other friends so I could slip out. Maybe I could even use JJ's "sickness" as an excuse that I wasn't feeling well.

"I was thinking you could meet me at my house at five. You can get dressed there and I'll do your hair and makeup."

Five! I needed to feed JJ. I wouldn't tell her, I'd just be a little late. "Okay but I'll just get dressed at home." I walked even faster so we could quit talking about the stupid party.

"I need to get there early because Alexa asked me to help with some stuff," she said.

"Fine. I'll meet you at Alexa's instead." I speed-walked to my locker, huffing by the time I got there. Ellen kept right up with me. She didn't even break stride.

"Ivy, don't make me go alone. You're my friend! I want you with me!"

What about what I want?

"Listen, I said I'll come, so I'll come. But I don't want to go that early and I don't want . . . to wear makeup." I hadn't really planned on saying the last part but out it came anyway.

Ellen pulled her skinny self up to her full height, poked out her scrawny chest, and said, "Ivy, I need you to be at my house at five o'clock tonight. Don't let me down or, I swear, you can find yourself another BFF."

She took off in a huff. Ellen had been my friend my whole life and she wasn't really asking that much of me. Especially since she'd bought me all that new stuff—even though I didn't want it. I owed her, so I'd have to go, but good grief, I did not want to. Not one tiny bit. I banged my head against my locker door. Brandon, whose locker was next to mine, said, "I don't think when people talk about banging their head against a wall, they mean it literally."

"Yeah, well those people probably aren't thinking that their life can't get any worse."

But I was wrong.

After school we walked home from the bus and I was just putting my key into the lock when the door opened. Standing inside, wearing an off-the-shoulder T-shirt and capris, with her dark hair streaked blond and tucked behind one ear showing about six earrings, was Aunt Maureen. That sounds like a good thing, right? And I thought so, too, at first. But how would you feel if you'd been working so hard to help your family and to keep things up and running, and then have your aunt hug you and say, "How could I stay away? Someone's got to be here to keep this sinking boat afloat."

"Mayonnaise," Aunt Maureen said with her hand out like a doctor asking for a scalpel. I found the jar and put it in her hand. She closed that cabinet door and opened another.

"Macaroni," she said. I looked through the sacks of food she'd brought until I found it.

"Really, Aunt Maureen, I can put this stuff away. I know where it all goes."

"I know you do, sweet pea. But I don't and I need to familiarize myself with this kitchen if I'm going to cook in it."

"Did Mama . . . did she know you were coming?"

"No!" She flashed her bleach-stripped, blinding white teeth at me. "But I thought, here I am, sitting at home— again—waiting on Sonny to come home. And what happens when he gets there? He sleeps most of the weekend until he hits the road come Monday. That's no life, sweet pea."

"For him or for you?" I asked.

She let out her bark of laughter that I loved. "Good question." She pulled a peppermint stick out of her purse and put it in her mouth, talking around it. "Not for me, that's for dang sure."

She pulled the stick out of her mouth and held it between her pointer and middle fingers, just like the cigarette she'd told me it was supposed to replace. "That's not the marriage I signed up for, let me tell you. Not one bit."

I thought about Uncle Sonny. I hadn't seen him in a long time but he always made me feel special. When he talked to me, you'd have thought I was the smartest and prettiest girl on the planet. And it wasn't just me. That's how he treated everyone. I wondered what kind of marriage Aunt Maureen wanted that would be better than being made to feel like that.

"But . . . Uncle Sonny is, well, so *lovable!*"

She got very busy in the cabinets. When she looked at me again, she said, "Yes, he is," and her voice quivered a little bit. "When he's there."

Then her voice got stronger. "Which is my point exactly. He's never there. Or almost never, anyway.

"So I'm sitting there thinking." She took a puff off her peppermint stick, made a face, and set it down. "I'm thinking that I have no one to cook for or look after and here your mama is with even more kids than she had once this divorce started and I'm all alone."

I'd heard Aunt Maureen cry to Mama about how she wasn't having any luck in getting pregnant.

"So I packed up my bags, called Sonny, and told him that the next time his big rig found its way home not to expect dinner, and here I am. Now hand me the sugar, sweet pea."

I took longer than I needed with my head in the sack but I was trying to figure out how I was going to get to Alexa's party now that Aunt Maureen was here.

In came JJ, riding on his sneakers with wheels. He circled the kitchen table once and then flew straight into Aunt Maureen, wrapping his arms around her tight.

"You'd *better* come see me, you little stinker. What do you think of those Heelys I bought you?"

"I *love* them! I'm giving you a hug every hour, Aunt Maureen, so you won't leave!"

She winked at me. "Gifts work every time."

"You didn't need to buy us anything," I said, but the

truth was, I really did like the iPod Shuffle she brought me. She even gave Caleb a gift card to a bookstore since she didn't know what kind of stuff he liked.

"Well, of course I did!" she said. "I plan to spoil you guys rotten. And don't you worry about me leaving, JJ. I'm not going anywhere. Now go get Caleb. It's time I got to know that boy."

I handed her the sugar but she set it down. "Oh, this can wait. Let me just soak you all up before your mama gets home and steals your attention."

I thought of how happy Mama had been this week, coming in with her face glowing, like getting away from us was the best thing that had ever happened to her. She might be tired, and she complained some about her feet hurting, but I knew Mama. I could tell she loved working. She didn't even seem to mind that she wasn't seeing JJ off to bed, and you know what? That hurt me almost as much as her not asking one single thing about me. I could have been expelled from school and she'd never have known.

We went into the living room and JJ came soaring in after us on his new shoes, with Caleb following. Aunt Maureen glided down onto the couch, reaching one long arm across the back. I always thought she could have been a ballerina the way she moved so gracefully. She patted the seat next to her.

"Come sit, Caleb. Tell me about yourself."

Good luck with that, I thought. I was starting to think that Caleb didn't know anything but made-up stories.

"How far did you travel, ma'am?" he asked.

"Halfway across the country! I was raised here in Indiana and just could not wait to shake the dust off my shoes and get out of here. Now look, I've come full circle. Couldn't wait to get back. I've been living in Georgia. You ever been there, Caleb?"

He shook his head, so she continued to tell him about her life in Georgia and I lost all interest. I knew the how-Aunt-Maureen-moved-to-Georgia story by heart, having heard it a million and one times from her and Mama, so I stood and tried to sneak upstairs to get to the phone in the hall there. I planned to call Ellen and tell her about Aunt Maureen's visit and maybe, just maybe, she'd let me off the hook about Alexa's party.

I got three steps up when I heard "Am I boring you, sweet pea?"

"What? No!" I said. "It's just that I . . ." Lying never came easy to me so I decided to saw off a slice of the truth. "I just need to call a friend."

"Well, why didn't you say so? Nothing's more important than girl-talk. You run along, honey. Dinner will be ready at six, okay?"

I smiled but I'll bet you dollars to doughnuts that my face made more of a grimace. Five o'clock was when I was supposed to be at Ellen's.

I took the stairs two at a time and punched in her number. Once she got on the phone I tried to get out of going but no such luck.

"You've got to be kidding me! I told you today how important this is to me, Ivy."

"It's just that Mama doesn't approve of boy-girl parties and I thought I could sneak out but now I've got my aunt Maureen here. I don't see how I can do it."

"Just do it," she said. "I don't give a rat's behind how you do it. If you were a real friend, you'd be over here right now helping me straighten my hair!"

Then she hung up. Slammed the phone down is more accurate. Ellen was always a little high-strung, but since she'd heard about this party, she'd been strung tighter than a guitar.

I threw myself down on my bed. What was I going to do?

Then I sat up. At five o'clock, Mama would still be at work, and Aunt Maureen didn't know that I wasn't supposed to go to a party. Heck, she probably wouldn't even ask where I was going. Or I could lie. Well, as I said, I wasn't very good at lying but I didn't need to go all out with the truth, either.

I changed into the clothes Ellen bought me and ran downstairs.

Aunt Maureen was in the kitchen stirring something in a pot and Caleb was peeling potatoes.

"There you are! My, Ivy, you didn't have to dress for dinner! JJ's job is to set the table—*without wearing his Heelys.*" She looked at him and raised her eyebrows. "Caleb is our potato person. You can be our salad maker."

"Okay," I said, and began yanking veggies out of the fridge. I grabbed a knife and quickly hacked up the lettuce.

"Whoa, girl! You're not killing snakes," she said. "Didn't your mama teach you how to make a salad?"

"She did. It's just that . . . my friend? The one I called? Well, she wants me to come over because she's . . . upset." Truth. Because if I didn't go, the word "upset" wouldn't begin to cover it. "So I guess I'm trying to hurry."

Aunt Maureen took the knife from my hand. "Ah! Boy trouble?"

I started to protest because Mama said she'd put me in an all girls' school if I even thought about boys, let alone dated one. But Aunt Maureen said, "There's nothing worse, honey. You just run on over there whenever you want. Let me make you a sandwich first."

She spread mayonnaise on whole wheat and layered turkey slices from the deli on it. My stomach growled and I dived right in when she handed it to me.

"Run along! Here, take a pop with you."

I smiled my thanks since my mouth was bulging with sandwich. It was so easy that I wondered why I had ever worried about it to begin with until she said, "Just be home by six-thirty, you hear?"

I nodded, glad this part was over and eager to leave. I turned to go and had to make my way around Caleb as he threw the potato peels into the trash can by the door.

He looked at me as if he could read my mind and a little chill ran down my spine.

11

Ellen tucked my hair behind my ear. Again. I yanked it out. Again. "It looks better that way!" she said. I ignored her because, really, how many different ways can you say "Leave me alone!" By my count I was up to about twelve.

She pulled a mirror out of her purse and checked her makeup. "Are you sure I look good?"

Again, how many times can you say something?

"Yeah, I'm sure."

Maybe she didn't believe me because my reassurance sounded fake even to my own ears. Her new boots weren't broken in so they were really stiff. Her jeans were snug and no girl with scrawny legs should wear skinny jeans unless she wants to be compared to walking chopsticks. But I kept my mouth shut so she wouldn't cry and ruin her eye makeup, which had taken her exactly eighteen minutes to get just right. I know. I timed her.

When we got to Alexa's, she stiff-walked her way to

the front door, panting. I thought maybe she couldn't breathe very well with those tight jeans until she squeezed my arm and squealed, "This is so exciting!"

Oh, yeah! I thought. *Almost as much fun as that pop quiz in math.*

Alexa opened the door and Ellen immediately stopped smiling. She put one hand on her jutted-out hip and said, "'Sup?"

Looking her up and down, Alexa said, "So you came."

"Of course. I said I would, didn't I?" Ellen walked past her like she owned the house. That left me standing on the porch.

Alexa eyed me as she leaned back against the opened screen door. "What do you want?"

That just burned me, so I said, "Pizza delivery. Except I got hungry and ate yours."

I wanted to leave right then but Ellen's face went completely white. "She's my guest," she said.

Alexa sneered. "When I said 'guest,' I meant boyfriend, but whatever." She swung her hip against the screen door so it opened even farther and walked into the house, leaving me to grab the door before it slammed shut.

She walked past Ellen like she wasn't even there. Ellen's face had gone from ghostly white to deep red and I felt sorry for her. She tried to smile but her lips shook a little. She whispered, "It's okay, Ivy. She didn't mean anything. Don't worry about it."

"I'm not worried!" My whisper was louder than hers

but I was mad. "You're the only one here who cares what she thinks."

Alexa started down the hall and looked back over her shoulder at Ellen. "Are you coming?"

Ellen mouthed to me, "I'll be back soon."

She turned and copied Alexa's slow, hip-rocking way of walking. Or tried to as best a skinny girl can in too-stiff boots. Just inside the front door was what was obviously the "party room." All the furniture was pushed against the walls and a table was covered in food. I walked in and picked up an MP3 player and went through the 300-plus songs on the playlist. I wanted to see if it worked the same way as the iPod Shuffle that Aunt Maureen got me. I sure felt lucky to have it. But then I remembered that the only thing Caleb owned was a box filled with notebooks and magazines. Not that I wanted to be thinking about Caleb but sometimes you can't control every thought that pops into your head.

Before I knew it, some girls from school arrived. They hung in groups, most of them looking as stiff and out of place as Ellen. And where *was* Ellen, anyway? Alexa had come out when the girls showed up but Ellen was no-where to be seen.

Then boys came and it seemed a little more fun, be-cause here's the thing about boys: they don't really care how they look. Oh, their mamas probably made them wear nice shirts and comb their hair and stuff but they didn't look like they were trying to be something they weren't, like the girls. So I loaded a plate of chips and dip and went over to stand by them.

It was awkward at first because someone started playing music and the boys got all self-conscious. Mainly because the girls lined up and eyed them like they had no choice but to come over and dance. So no one did anything for a while, just girls on one side waiting, boys (and me) on the other fidgeting. Well, the boys fidgeted. I ate. Then I think the boys probably just decided to do what they do best: talk sports.

"How much do you practice?" Brandon asked Andrew. They'd both been in my grade since preschool.

"I don't. I just play backyard ball," Andrew said.

"You have to practice, moron. This is junior high. Cuts are made in football now. It's not like last year when we all got to play. *I'm* not going to be cut or sit on the bench."

"How much do you practice then?"

"I throw passes in my sleep." And to demonstrate, Brandon closed his eyes and pretended to spiral a ball out of his hand.

"If you're asleep, that explains why you're so bad," Andrew said. All the guys laughed and so did I.

"We'll see which one of us is sitting and which is playing, Andrew."

"Awake or asleep?" Andrew said, and let out a fake snore that almost shook the house.

Alexa came over to the boys and rubbed Brandon's arm. "Aw, don't listen. We know you're wonderful. Come sit by me."

But Brandon didn't seem to care that she was there. He shrugged her hand away and took a step back. He was close to me and moved so suddenly that I jumped, causing chips to hop off my plate. That sounds like something that only happens on TV shows but I found out you can be so startled that you really do it.

"Oh!" I said.

"Ugh! Look what you did!" Alexa pointed to my mess.

"My bad," Brandon said, but Alexa stalked off toward the kitchen.

Brandon crouched down to help me pick up the chips. He had on one of those watches with the big dials and I saw that it looked like it was twelve o'clock. I grabbed his arm and tilted my head so the watch wasn't upside down. Six-thirty!

"I'm sorry! I . . . I've got to go," I stammered. I made my way through the crowd and had reached the front door when Alexa came dragging Ellen into the room. Ellen was pulling yellow rubber gloves on and her once perfectly straightened hair was curling from sweat. Under her arm was tucked a hand broom and dustpan.

All this flashed through my mind in a millisecond as I tried to get out the door. I'd almost made it when a girl I didn't know pointed to me and asked, "Who is she?"

Alexa looked at me and said, "Her? She's Ellen's date."

I blasted through the door just as a wave of laughter washed over the room. I didn't dare look back at Ellen.

Running through the alley, I held on to the hope that I'd beat Mama home, but when the house came into view, there was Mama's car. I was almost to my front door when Caleb came out of nowhere and grabbed my arm, pulling me off the sidewalk into the yard.

"Let go, freak!" I yelled.

"Shhh!" he said.

"Shoosh yourself! And don't *ever* grab me like that again!"

"Listen," he said, and then lowered his voice to a whisper. "You've been home. You found a bird's nest on the ground out back. You were keeping guard until the baby birds flew away."

He thrust a nest into my hand. At that moment Aunt Maureen and Mama came out onto the porch.

"Young lady," Aunt Maureen said, "you're late!"

"What's this about?" Mama asked. "Ivy, where have you been?"

I hesitated for a minute, then the words came out of my mouth on their own. "I've been home. I found a bird's nest on the ground out back. I've been keeping guard until the baby birds flew away."

Mama looked at the nest in my hand. Her face softened because Mama loved all living things so. "Why,

Ivy! What a sweet thing to do. Come here, you." She wrapped her arms around me in a hug.

My head spun a little. I think it was because so much had happened in such a short time. I should have been mad at Caleb for a lot of things. I should have been ashamed of myself for lying. I should have worried that I hadn't already shown Mama my new clothes. But all I knew was that Mama was hugging me and I wasn't in trouble and it was a really nice feeling.

"Come inside." She took the nest from me and set it in a bush, put her arm around me, and led me up the steps and into the living room. "Can you *believe* your aunt Maureen is here? I don't think I've ever been happier."

"Then you lead one boring life, Cass." Aunt Maureen looked at Mama and raised her eyebrows. "Besides, my memory is good and I know for a fact you've had some happier moments. Just none that are G-rated."

She and Mama both broke into loud laughter.

"JJ's in his room playing so all you have to do is get over here and take a load off while Ivy, Caleb, and I do the dishes."

Mama raised her feet onto the couch and sighed. "I'd argue but I'm too tired and grateful."

Caleb followed Aunt Maureen into the kitchen. "Be right there!" I called, and ran upstairs to get out of the clothes Ellen had bought me before Mama noticed them. When I headed to the kitchen, I passed Mama but her eyes were closed and she had a small smile on her face.

In the kitchen, Aunt Maureen already had the sink filled with soapy water.

"Caleb, you bring us the dirty dishes. I'll wash," she said. "Ivy will dry and put them away."

Then she lowered her voice. "And while we're all nice and busy, you'll both tell me what that bird lie was about."

Caleb and I froze. Aunt Maureen let out a low, barklike laugh. "Kids, I am not Cass Henry. I don't get all dewy-eyed over a baby bird story and I can smell a lie a mile away. You're not in trouble yet and I won't tell Cass unless it involves a dead body or stealing, but you *are* going to spill the beans."

Before I could say anything, Caleb jumped in. "I found the nest, ma'am."

"And that's all well and good but that doesn't explain why Ivy was late, now does it, Caleb?"

"I'm sorry, Aunt Maureen. I should have watched the time more."

"And what exciting things were you doing that made time fly?" she asked.

"Well . . ." I gulped. "I did go see my friend, just like I told you."

"And?"

I wondered how it was possible for her to look at me so long and not blink.

"And . . ." I weighed my options. She said she wouldn't

tell Mama but I knew there wasn't much she and Mama didn't share. My mind was totally blank. I couldn't think of any good excuse for being late. Besides that, I was tired of lying. I kept catching everyone else in lies and here I was, doing it, too.

"I went to a party." I told the truth but I couldn't look her in the eye.

"Did something happen at this party?"

"No, not really."

"So what's the problem then?" she asked.

"There were boys there."

"It wouldn't be much of a party if there weren't."

"Mama won't let me go to parties with boys." I kept my head down and my hair covered my hot face.

"Is this a joke?" she asked, putting one hand on her hip. "Cass Henry won't let her daughter go to parties with boys?"

"No, ma'am. It's no joke," I said.

Then she let loose with a loud laugh. Mama's voice came in from the living room. "Don't y'all be having so much fun without me."

Here it comes, I thought, and braced for Aunt Maureen to tell Mama why she'd laughed. But she said, "You just rest, Cass. I'm only laughing at how clumsy I am tonight. I've got a case of the dropsies." She lowered her voice again, crossed her arms over her chest, and leaned back against the sink. "So, like mother like daughter."

"I'm like Mama?" I asked.

She tilted her head left to right, like she couldn't decide. "More like Cass is like her mother."

"Mama sneaked out for parties?" I asked. This didn't fit with the Mama I knew but I guess I'd never heard her talk to Aunt Maureen about what it was like to be my age.

"I don't want to go there, Ivy. That's up to your mom. Just answer me this. Did you kiss a boy tonight?"

"No!" I said, absolutely horrified.

"Are you sure?"

"Aunt Maureen! I didn't even want to be there! I was afraid of losing Ellen as my friend if I didn't go and that's the truth."

She pushed up off the sink and said, "Then I see no reason your mama needs to know. I'm not saying you should disobey her but we've all been in spots like you are in now, Ivy. But you tell your Aunt Maureen the truth, young lady. If I ask where you're going, I damn well want to know."

"Yes, ma'am."

"And I think your goose would have been cooked with your mother if Caleb hadn't stepped in to help. He even told her he knew you were home before you really were. So I suppose you owe him, but, Caleb." Her eyes slid to him. "I'm giving you the same warning I told Ivy. Don't lie to me again, young man."

Good luck with that, I thought. But I bit my tongue. After all, he'd lied to help me. Not that I wanted his help, you understand. Not at all. But, still . . .

12

Later that night, Mama and Aunt Maureen were curled up on each end of the couch, their hands wrapped around coffee mugs. A person would think that, as much talking as they did on the phone, there wouldn't be anything left to talk about, but they were deep in discussion when Caleb and I went upstairs to get ready for bed.

"Caleb, wait," I said. "You've got me confused. Why did you help me?"

"Your mother was upset."

"That's not what I asked."

"I knew you were going to the party, and I also knew that, if you told your aunt you'd be home by six-thirty, you'd do your best."

"How did you know about the party? Have you been spying on me?"

"When things are said in front of you, is hearing them considered spying?" he asked.

I thought about his question and about how Mama

was always talking to Aunt Maureen in front of me. Sure, it was spying when I picked up the phone and listened, but I didn't think it was spying when I was in the same room and she said things that I heard.

"No, I don't think that's spying."

"You talked to Ellen on the phone about the party. I went upstairs to put my gift card in my room before helping with dinner and I heard you. I wasn't spying."

"But that's not all," I said. "You also had a ready-made excuse for me to not get into trouble."

"My parents . . . they always tried to help people. That's what I do now. I try to help."

"If you wanted to help so dang much and you knew I was at Alexa's, why didn't you come and get me?"

He looked down at his feet. I wondered if he was ever going to answer me but then he said, "Do you really think anyone there would have let me in?"

Would they? I pushed the question out of my mind but not before I realized that the answer was no, they probably wouldn't have.

You'd think a person should be able to sleep in on a Saturday but, as I mentioned before, not in our house. I woke to a buzzing sound and I reached for my alarm clock. I hit the snooze button, but it kept going. I reached again and knocked it off the table, sending it *kerthunking* onto the floor.

I groaned and woke up enough to pull it by the cord

back onto the table. That's when I realized the sound I heard was the doorbell. I rolled out of bed and made it halfway downstairs when I heard Aunt Maureen talking through the screen door. It was pretty easy to see by her mussed hair and silk robe that whoever had come calling had woken her, too.

I squatted on the step and listened.

"Now, I don't want to be mean but we don't want any pamphlets if you really are from a church. I thought you boys traveled in pairs with white shirts and backpacks."

"I'm not a Mormon!"

"Well, I really don't care what church you're from. If we want to go to church, we'll find one. Goodbye."

She started to shut the door.

"Wait! Mrs. Henry knows about this." It was Pastor Harold's voice.

"Well now, I was up half the night with *Ms*. Henry and she didn't say anything about going to church on Saturday."

I raced down the steps. "He's right, Aunt Maureen! Mama told him she'd work at the church kitchen this morning."

"Oh, for heaven's sake. I'm going back to bed," she said.

"Come on in, Pastor Harold. I'll get Mama."

He stepped inside and I raced past Aunt Maureen on the stairs. Mama wasn't in her room so I knocked on the bathroom door.

"Mama! It's nine o'clock and Pastor Harold is here.

You told him you'd be ready to work at the church at nine. Remember?"

Mama opened the door, tying the sash on her robe. "Oh my goodness! Go stall him for me."

I ran back downstairs. "She's getting ready now, Pastor Harold. Want me to get you some coffee?"

"Sure, coffee would be nice."

I hurried into the kitchen and pushed the button on the coffeemaker since Mama always put the water and coffee grounds in the night before. Then I got down a mug and the sugar bowl.

"You can sit while it brews," I said.

"Thank you." He pulled out a chair and smiled at me. "You're a good hostess."

Which made me feel way better than it probably should have.

"Don't pay any mind to Aunt Maureen. She just got here from Georgia. She's been Mama's friend for eons." I was glad to use a word that made me sound like a "hostess" instead of a kid in an outgrown nightgown.

"Oh, that's fine. No one likes to be woken up. I know I don't."

I poured coffee into his cup and he nodded his thanks.

"By the way, is Caleb around?" he asked. "I'd like to talk to him."

"He's probably still in bed like I was."

"So I woke you, too? And you're even nice about it." His eyes had those little crinkles in the corners again.

I set the pot back on the warmer so it would stay hot for Mama. "Well, I'm sure my mom will be back shortly. I'll go get dressed now."

And I took off. I met Mama in the hall, smoothing a sweatshirt down over her jeans.

"Do I look all right?" she asked.

"For making noodles? Who cares?"

"Well, I care!"

"You could wear your pajamas to make noodles with old ladies, Mama."

"They're not all old ladies, Ivy. And Pastor Harold will be there."

"So?"

"So, I'm just saying I want to look nice, that's all," she said as she hurried on past me.

The phone rang and Aunt Maureen groaned from the bedroom she was sharing with Mama. "Good Lord, this place is a zoo!"

I quickly picked it up and whispered, "Hello."

"I just wanted to say thanks for *nothing*, Ivy." It was Ellen. "Because of you, everyone thinks I'm a lesbian. And not only that, you ran out on me last night!"

"But neither one of us knew that 'guest' meant boyfriend, Ellen!"

She started bawling. There's no getting through to her when she's a mess like that.

"How about I come over and we can talk about it?" I said.

"Don't bother! If you couldn't stay when I needed you, what good does it do me now?"

"Oh, come on, Ellen! I went to the party, didn't I? I mean, I had to leave before you, but still, I came. And it's not like you cared that I was there, anyway. You weren't even around."

"I *told* you I had to help!"

"Help do what? Clean up messes? That's not what guests do."

"You have no idea how hard it is to be in Alexa's group, do you? You have to earn that spot and you just thought you'd sail into it through me. Well, Ivy, I don't need you. I don't want to be seen with you ever again!"

And she hung up the phone! I just kept talking, saying stuff like "Wait a minute!" and "You can't hang up like that!" which was stupid because she wasn't there to hear me. And who cared about Alexa's "group"? I didn't even know she had a *group*. It sounded like she was lead singer in a band or something, not just the queen of a dumb bunch of girls who followed her around. Why would I want to be part of that?

I was brushing my teeth when the phone rang again. I spit and ran into the hall, ready to give Ellen a piece of my mind, when I heard Aunt Maureen's voice.

"I told you I wouldn't be there, Sonny . . . Yes, I know I've threatened before but this time it's different. Cass needs me. And, honestly, even if she didn't, things haven't been good between you and me for quite a while."

I peeked around the corner and she was leaning against the wall, her pajamas still on.

"Oh, Sonny. You know I loved you. I probably still do but I can't come back. I'm so lonely and you're never there. I just can't go on this way." She hung up the phone and wiped tears from under her eyes. I hurried to the bathroom, hung my toothbrush on the rack, then met her in the hall.

"Morning, sunshine. Is it always this busy around here?"

Her eyes were red and she sounded like she had a cold but I pretended not to notice. "Not usually."

"Thank gawd! I don't think I could take it."

She tried to act like the fun Aunt Maureen, the one who didn't care about anything. Like her heart wasn't broken, but I knew it was. I had a queasy feeling in my stomach for both her and Uncle Sonny—just like I did when Jack Henry broke Mama's heart.

I washed the breakfast dishes since Aunt Maureen had cooked. She had Caleb running the sweeper and JJ dusting the big, unbreakable pieces of furniture, which was a miracle in itself. When we finished, JJ asked Caleb to go with him to see the "hungry Haitians" by Harmony Street Blues.

"Who?" I asked.

"The people Daddy showed me. The ones who don't have houses or money."

"They don't have houses so that means they're homeless, JJ. You have no business going there at all, not even with Caleb."

"You're mean!" JJ called as he ran outside.

I turned to Caleb. "You go get him. You're the one putting ideas in his head."

Caleb left, and through the open door I saw Pastor Harold's silver ball of a car pull up. He got out and opened Mama's door for her. I watched them from the window. Mama leaned back against his car and smiled a lot. Then they both really laughed. They talked a bit longer and then she must have asked him in. I jumped back from the window, flopped down on the couch, and grabbed a magazine like I'd been reading it instead of trying to read their lips.

"Have a seat," Mama said. "I'll get that iced tea."

I looked over the top of the magazine. Pastor Harold chuckled.

"What's so funny?" I asked.

He lifted the magazine out of my hands and rotated it.

"It might read easier right side up," he said.

I felt my face getting warm.

"That's okay. Spying on grownups was always my favorite pastime, too."

"I don't spy!" I said.

"Well, paying attention to them," he said. "How's that?"

"I haven't seen any grownups come around here who are worth paying attention to," I said.

He laughed. "Ivy, you're all right."

"So I've been told."

"Maybe you haven't been paying attention to me but I have to you. I listened to your concerns about Caleb."

"Yeah?"

"Yeah. I decided that, interim pastor or no, I should know more about my flock."

Mama came in with three glasses of iced tea. "Where's Maureen?"

"Upstairs, I think," I said.

I about fell over when she handed me a glass. But then she ruined it by saying, "Well, go get her, please. And give her that tea."

My jaw dropped and my mouth hung open. I set the glass down on the table with a bang and went looking for Aunt Maureen.

"If you're going to ignore my instructions, Ivy, you could at least use a coaster!" Mama called after me.

I found Aunt Maureen sitting on the bed, plugged into her iPod and filing her nails. I waved my hand in front of her face to get her attention.

"Mama wants you downstairs." I kept the sour look on my face.

"My what an attitude you have," she drawled. She slid

her long legs over the side and stretched like a cat. "Keep that up and the crown for Miss Congeniality will definitely be yours."

Deep down I knew I wasn't mad at her, just Mama, but right then I was angry and sometimes that makes you mad at everybody you see.

Aunt Maureen followed me downstairs. Pastor Harold looked up. "Ivy, I was just telling your mom about something that I could use your help with."

"Me?"

"Unless there's another girl named Ivy in the room." He held out his glass. "Maybe you could get yourself one of these and join us."

I beat it into the kitchen, thankful that at least Pastor Harold had noticed that I got left out. There was just enough tea left for me. I even thought about adding a slice of lemon, this being sort of an occasion and all, but why ruin a good glass of tea with a bitter piece of fruit?

I carried it back into the room and Pastor Harold continued, "As I was saying, this stove burns corn. It was a parting gift from the last church I served."

"Seems like an odd gift for someone who makes their living moving from place to place," Mama said.

He chuckled. "I guess that's true. It was a poor parish. Somebody probably had it and didn't know what to do with it. But, you know, it's the thought that counts, right? Anyway, I just have an apartment and, as you said, I move around so it won't do me any good. I'd be happy to come and install it. It would make heating this house much more affordable."

"I'm all for that," Mama said. "I hadn't let myself think ahead to this fall. But is it safe? I'm not sure how it even works."

"I guess the simplest way to explain it is that it works much like a wood-burning stove only you feed it dried corn. Like this." He pulled a pen out of his shirt pocket and found a scrap of paper in his pants. He began drawing a picture and Mama scooted over to see it. They put their heads together and murmured softly.

I took a drink of my tea, then looked over at Aunt Maureen. She was frowning as if she didn't like them being so close. I wondered what the big deal was. I mean, it was just Pastor Harold.

At one point, though, he looked at Mama, she looked at him, and they both pulled back like they'd been caught doing something wrong.

Pastor Harold cleared his throat and said in a voice loud enough to include us all, "It burns cleaner, doesn't cost much at all, and you don't have to chop and stack wood. You just carry buckets of corn in. I'm sure your kids would be great helpers."

"Where would I get corn?" Mama asked.

"I can find lots of sources for you, feed stores, farmers, et cetera. I can even deliver it in my old pickup. Corn is cheap and I think you'll get a really good deal from the delivery guy." He winked.

"I'm here now and I'll be sharing the expenses," Aunt Maureen said. "I don't know if you want to fool with something like that."

"It's my house, Maureen. You're not paying my bills for me."

"Now, Cass," she said. "I'm not staying here for free."

"And we don't even know if the landlord will allow it." Mama set her glass on a coaster. "If you'll excuse me, I'll call him now. No point in discussing something that might not happen anyway."

Pastor Harold said, "Well, I'll let you all decide, but, Ivy, if I do install it, will you help me?"

"Me?" There I went again. Just repeating the same dumb word. He was going to think I wasn't smarter than a parrot.

"Sure," he said. "I'll need someone to hand me tools. Maybe Caleb could help, too. In fact, is he around?"

"No, he left with JJ," I said.

"You're building up quite an army of helpers for something that hasn't been decided yet," Aunt Maureen said.

"I just like to be prepared," Pastor Harold said, and I noticed his eyes didn't have the same spark when he talked to Aunt Maureen as they did when he talked to me or Mama.

"A regular boy scout." She sipped her tea. "Always prepared."

Mama came back into the room. "You seem to have

quite a reputation as a handyman! I called Mr. Morgan and he said he felt comfortable with you installing it."

Pastor Harold gave a slow smile. "Well, I do a bit of carpentry. I've found myself in between churches with some downtime and it's nice to have a backup occupation. The forecast is calling for some pretty cold nights. I think it's safe to say we're heading into autumn. If you decide you want the stove, I'm free any evening this week."

"Doesn't sound like you have much of a social life, being free every night." Aunt Maureen lit a for-real ciga- rette instead of sucking on a peppermint stick, which told me she was agitated.

"It's lucky for us he's not busy this week," Mama said to her with *feeling*, which shut Aunt Maureen up because even she knew not to cross Mama.

"Thanks for the tea, Cass." Pastor Harold surprised me when he called Mama by her first name. "And I'm sure the ladies of the Guild appreciated your help."

Mama laughed. "I don't think I was much help. They had a regular assembly line going. I'm still not sure why they needed me."

"Look at it this way, they only gossip about the ones who aren't there."

Mama held her hand over her mouth and laughed. I hadn't seen her do that since Jack Henry was around. I could tell by the look on Aunt Maureen's face that she had noticed it, too.

13

Pastor Harold had treated me like a grownup, which was something the other grownups in the house could do more often, in my opinion. So I followed him out.

"Hey," I said. "I don't know about Caleb but I'll help you."

"Glad to hear it." He smiled.

"And I just wanted to say . . . I mean . . . I don't hate you or anything."

He laughed real loud. "Ivy, you're—"

"I know," I interrupted. "I'm all right. All I meant is, earlier when I said there weren't any adults worth paying attention to, well, I know that sounded kind of snotty."

"Aw, you're entitled to your opinion. Adults, for the most part, are pretty boring."

He pushed a button on his keychain that beeped and unlocked his car.

I went on before he could climb inside. "And the other day, well, maybe I shouldn't have yelled at you for not knowing more about Caleb. I didn't know you were just a temporary pastor and all."

"You don't owe me an apology. You were right, I need to know these things if I'm going to do a good job here. No harm done."

"And I don't know why Aunt Maureen isn't nicer to you, too. She's usually a pretty kind person."

"Well, she's not exactly mean to me, just a little on the cool side," he said. "Maybe my sunny disposition will win her over. And, if not, I'll rise above it."

It made me think of Ellen and how mad she was at me.

"How does a person rise above someone not liking them?"

He folded his arms across his chest and leaned against his car. "That's a tough one. It was my dad's favorite saying. I guess you have to strive for the greater good." He ran his hands over his short hair. "Oh, great, now I sound like a preacher."

Which I thought was kind of funny.

"It mainly means that when someone forms an inaccurate opinion of you, the best you can do is just be yourself and try not to let it get to you. So I guess that's what I mean about rising above and striving for the greater good and all that."

It gave me something to think about the next few days.

I tried to rise above lots of things. I tried to rise above JJ wanting to always be with Caleb instead of with me. I rose to my fullest with Aunt Maureen running the house, even tucking JJ into bed at night. But my striving for the greater good was put to the test when I saw Ellen at school on Monday and she acted as if she didn't even know me.

It's hard to go from being someone's BFF to feeling invisible.

Want to know what made it even harder? I never expected Ellen to do anything other than hang out with me and have fun. But, with Alexa, Ellen was doing so much work! First there was Alexa's party. Who invites someone to a party and expects them to be a maid? Then, during lunch at school, I noticed that Ellen got Alexa's tray of food and brought it to her while Alexa talked to her other friends. When Ellen got her own food, she sat on the edge of the group—with them but not quite one of them, if you know what I mean.

It hurt to know that Ellen would rather be on the fringes of Alexa's group than sit with me. She wouldn't talk to me at all. I tried to sit with the boys in my class but it seemed that lots of social rules were different in seventh grade. I could hang out on their side of the room at Alexa's party and that was just fine, but when I walked toward their table, they all looked at me as if I had three heads. So I did the only thing I could. I sat with Lindsay. The one thing about sitting with Lindsay is you don't have to worry about holding up your end of the conversation. She does that for you. In fact, she held up the conversation until we had to go to different classes.

After the longest week of my entire life, Friday rolled around. Caleb, JJ, and I got home to find Mama already there.

"Mama!" JJ called, and ran to hug her.

"Did you lose your job?" I asked.

She rolled her eyes. "It's nice to see you, too, Ivy."

"Well, you're never here," I said. *Never, ever here.*

"A lot of things happened," she said. "Aunt Maureen is off getting her hair done. Pastor Harold called and needed to be let in to install the new stove."

"He's here?" I said, tossing my books onto the coffee table. "I didn't know he was coming."

JJ said, "Come on, Caleb! Let's find Pastor Harold!"

Mama said, "I guess he told Aunt Maureen and she must have forgotten. Anyway, he called me at work so Magdalena let me come home early."

"You'll be here tonight?" I said, and immediately hated the excited way it came out.

"No, that's another thing that happened. Aunt Maureen got tickets for the two of us to go to Indianapolis and see OLG in concert. It's a band that we loved when we were younger."

"Oh . . ."

"Well, girls, what do you think?" Aunt Maureen's voice carried into the room. She stood in the door, one arm raised and her head turned sideways in a model's pose.

"Oh, Maureen! You look incredible!" Mama said.

"You look awesome, Aunt Maureen!" I said, because she really did. Her hair was dyed blond and swept over her right eye but it was cut short over her left ear, showing off her earrings.

"I just decided it's time for a change. And what's the point of having all this ear jewelry if my hair keeps falling down over it?"

"I'm going to look downright dowdy next to you!" Mama said.

"Have no fear, Cass." Aunt Maureen held up a shopping bag. "Together we'll be the hottest babes there."

My mother? A hot babe?

Mama giggled.

I wanted to puke.

Then it hit me. Indianapolis is over an hour away. With Aunt Maureen gone, I'd be in charge again.

I shoved the "hot babe" comment out of my head and said, "Well, we'll be just fine here. You don't have to worry about us."

"Oh, that preacher's going to take care of you," Aunt Maureen said.

"Huh?"

"I talked to him earlier. He said he didn't mind."

Mama stopped smiling. "You remembered he was coming?"

"Uh-huh." Aunt Maureen bent to gather her purse and bags from the floor.

"Maureen, I had to take off work to let him in. I had no idea he was installing the stove today."

Aunt Maureen stood and looked straight at Mama. "Well, then, it all worked out, didn't it? Besides, you're home early so we can have more time to get ready. Where's the harm?"

"Where's the . . ." Mama seemed at a loss for words. "Maureen, when you said you'd arrange for a sitter, we discussed the kids I knew from church who I thought were trustworthy."

"Kids?! Mama, why would you get somebody my age to watch us?"

"They're older than you, Ivy. And it's fine for you and Caleb to watch over JJ when I'm at work here in town but Indianapolis is so far away. I just don't feel comfortable leaving you without someone else here."

Then she turned to Aunt Maureen. "Did you even call those girls?"

"I tried. Seems teenagers lead a busier life than we do. Besides, I figured he'd be here, anyway, putting that stove in."

"Isn't he doing enough for us?" Mama's eyes narrowed. "What have you got against him?"

"Me? Nothing. I don't know the man."

"And yet you have that attitude. He's trying to help me. It was your idea for me to go to church for help, remember?"

I stood still as a statue. I didn't want to miss this conversation.

"Yes, Cass, for help. That's one of the things churches are for."

And hearing her say that made me feel so much better about both Mama and Aunt Maureen. I'd thought they were using the people of the church in a bad way instead of just reaching out for help. But then Aunt Maureen said, "I wanted you to go and find a job, not for you to settle for a dull, Bible-toting preacher. It's time you had some fun in your life."

I sucked in my breath. I didn't mean to make a sound, but it was too late. Both of them looked right at me.

"Ivy Greer! Get your behind outside with the boys, *now*!" And I took off because Mama used the one tone of voice I knew from experience not to argue with.

I found Pastor Harold around back, trying to fit a pipe into a hole he'd put in the roof while Caleb steadied his ladder.

"There's my other helper now. Hey, Ivy."

"Hey," I said.

"So will we get sick now?" JJ asked.

"Sick? I surely hope not," Pastor Harold said.

"But you said you're putting the flu in and the last time we had the flu, Mama, Ivy, and I were all really sick."

Pastor Harold looked away so JJ wouldn't see him laughing. When he did, he saw me and winked. Then he wiped his face on his shirt and, afterward, his expression had changed to a serious one. "Actually, JJ, that's a different kind of flu. Smoke and carbon dioxide are produced when something burns, and you don't want that in your house. This flue is a pipe that lets those things out."

"Do they have flues in Haiti, Caleb? Do they have the kind that makes them sick or do they have the kind that takes the bad stuff out of their house? Or their huts. Because they have huts instead of houses, right, Caleb?"

Caleb took his hand off the ladder long enough to push his glasses back up. He ignored JJ, which wasn't like him at all, and I noticed his face was paler than usual.

"Come on, Caleb, they have huts, right?" he asked.

"Yes," Caleb said.

"And do they get sick with the flu?" JJ asked. Then he whined, "Come *on*, Caleb! Tell me. You've always got a story."

"JJ? I need your help," Pastor Harold said.

"Okay," JJ said.

"This is a very important job. Maybe *the* most important. I need someone to stay in the house and make sure that no birds fly in through the flue until I get it sealed. Do you think you can do that?"

"Wow! Sure! Can I get my net first? Just in case one gets in?"

"Absolutely. Go find your net and take your time." Pastor Harold looked at the sky. "I think we're safe for a bit. I don't see any birds right now."

"Okay!" JJ ran off.

"Hold that ladder, Caleb. I'm coming down."

Pastor Harold swung his leg over on the ladder and climbed down it like a pro. I thought he made a better carpenter than a preacher, but since he was doing us a favor, I decided that saying that might be kind of rude.

Once he reached ground, he said to Caleb, "I have a toolbox in the back of my truck with a pair of tin snips in it. Think you could go get them for me while I take a break?"

"Sure," Caleb said, and loped off.

Pastor Harold wore a troubled look on his face as he watched him go.

"What's up?" I asked.

"Nothing much. What's up with you?" he said.

"No, I mean, what's going on with Caleb? I saw the way you got rid of JJ when he was bothering him."

"Oh, maybe that's something I should talk to Caleb about. I'll go do that now, if you don't mind."

Then he headed for his truck. I don't know why but I felt sort of cold when he left. Like the sun had just gone behind a cloud. I saw him put his hand on Caleb's back and bend down so their heads were even. I kicked a rock, thinking, *Fine! Who cares, anyway?* I sure wasn't going to hang around to be sent on some fake job like keeping birds out of the house.

I went inside and walked by our extra room. It's what would be a dining room if we were the kind of family who "dined." We weren't, so it's the room Mama used to set up her ironing board, and JJ's LEGOs were spread around the floor. In the corner was the new stove Pastor Harold had brought. JJ was there, flipping his net in the air "catching" fake birds. I walked on by and picked up my bookbag to go upstairs and do my homework so I'd get it over with for the weekend.

Halfway to my room I heard Mama and Aunt Maureen giggling from Mama's bedroom. You'd never have known they were being all snippy to each other before. I shook my head and then buried it in my math book.

When I finally came up for air, I was really hungry. I put my books away and went for a snack, but I stopped dead in my tracks when I walked into the kitchen.

There was Mama; only it wasn't like I'd ever seen her. She had on a dress that was held up by two little straps, showing off her shoulders. Her hair was really straight and shiny. It looked so soft and it kind of flew out a little when she moved her head. She had on makeup and, well, she looked better than a movie star.

"Wow, Mama. You look beautiful," I said.

She smiled. "Thank you, sweetheart. I don't know about all that, though."

"No, she's right." It was Pastor Harold. He'd walked up behind me and I hadn't heard his footsteps. "Absolutely beautiful, Cass."

Mama's lips parted a little and her eyes got all soft. Pastor Harold looked like a guy who'd seen his first meal after a weeklong fast.

"Hark! It's Harold," Aunt Maureen said. "Now if just the angels'd sing."

We all laughed because she said it in a joking way, not a mean one like before.

"You look lovely, too, Maureen," he said.

"Well, thank you," she said. "I do try. How's that stove coming?"

"Pretty good. Almost done," he said, then his eyes went back to Mama.

"I can't tell you how much I appreciate all you've done for us," she said.

He whispered, "You're welcome." And the look he gave Mama made her pretty face turn pink. She fiddled with her hair, then looked at her wrist. "Oh my goodness, I forgot my watch. I'll be right back."

Pastor Harold watched Mama walk away. Aunt Maureen rolled her eyes and said, "I have a question for you, Harold. When's the last time you had a good meal?"

"Home-cooked? It's been a while," he said.

"I've made a batch of stew and it's delicious, if I do say so myself," Aunt Maureen said.

"It sounds wonderful!" he said.

"Great! Cass and I are leaving now."

"You ladies aren't staying to eat with us?" he asked.

"No, we're having dinner first with an old classmate, Derek. He and I have kept in touch over the years and he lives right there in Indianapolis. He's bringing his friend for Cass. Or, who knows? Maybe I'll end up without a date. They may both want her, as pretty as she looks to-night."

Pastor Harold looked confused at first. Then his eyes narrowed. "I see."

Just then Mama came back into the room. "I'll give you Maureen's cell phone number. I'm afraid I don't have one." She wrote it on the refrigerator door grocery list. "We'll try not to be late. JJ's bedtime is eight. Please don't even think about the dishes. You and the kids have worked so hard today. I'll get them in the morning."

He didn't look at Mama. "Well, you ladies have a nice time. I'll see to it that JJ is in bed at eight."

He turned and left the room.

"Are you ready, Cass?" Aunt Maureen said.

"I don't know," Mama said. "I feel bad, Maureen. He's here to help and we're taking advantage of him."

Aunt Maureen put her hand on Mama's arm. "We've been through this. You deserve a night out. He's here, anyway. He's getting a nice meal out of it, and if you don't believe that, then you've never had my stew. Now let's get going. We don't want to be late."

Mama kissed me on the forehead. "Here's an early goodnight kiss." Then she went to say goodbye to JJ and Caleb. I hoped she did the same to Pastor Harold. Tell him goodbye, I mean, not give him a kiss.

"Sugar, don't stay up too late," Aunt Maureen said. "Try to keep the noise to a dull roar in the morning, okay?

And lock the doors tonight. Your mama and I won't be home until the wee small hours!"

"But Mama said you wouldn't be late."

"Mama forgets what it's like to have a good time." She spun and danced her way out of the room, throwing me a wink as she left. I wasn't really crazy about the way Aunt Maureen was acting. I preferred the old Aunt Maureen. The one who was nice to everybody, including Uncle Sonny. Then I felt guilty. She came all this way to help us—whether or not I thought we needed her help was beside the point. She did work hard here and she sure made Mama happy.

Caleb and JJ helped Pastor Harold put away his tools and ladder while I warmed the stew. Pastor Harold sat back and moaned after the first bite. "Oh, wow. This has to be the best stew I've ever eaten." Then he dug in. I hadn't cooked it and didn't make any claim to have helped. But I did warm it so his liking it made me feel like I *had* cooked it.

He even did the dishes afterward while I put the leftover stew away. He didn't have to do that, since Mama had told him not to, but I didn't try to stop him, either.

"Okay." He rubbed his hands together and looked at the clock. "Seven-thirty. Ivy, what's next on the to-do list?"

"It's JJ's bath and then bed," I said.

"I'll bet you're a big help to your mom. You probably know how to handle your brother."

I looked down so that stupid grin wouldn't take over my face again.

"I do all right," I said.

"So how about you take care of JJ while Caleb and I take out the trash?"

"Okay!"

It felt good taking care of JJ again. I had more patience with him than I used to. I poured bubble bath in the tub and we took turns making bubble beards on our faces. Then I tucked him into bed and he fell asleep almost immediately, no story needed.

I came out of JJ's room, expecting to find Pastor Harold and Caleb downstairs, but they were in Caleb's room, both sitting on the side of his bed, looking through Caleb's books. It felt like they had some big secret that I wasn't a part of.

I went downstairs and flipped on the television. When Pastor Harold finally came downstairs, I pretended I'd fallen asleep. He covered me with the throw that was spread over the back of the couch and turned the television off. It was kind of a lie, me pretending to be asleep. But it was better than the truth, which was that I felt left out.

Suddenly my eyes snapped open. That's exactly how Caleb would have felt at Alexa's party. So, I strove for the greater good and said, "Thanks for all you did today."

"You're welcome," he whispered.

He probably thought I just meant the stove.

14

JJ dropped his cup at breakfast the next morning. It broke, spraying milk and glass shards everywhere. Mama and I jumped up to grab paper towels but Aunt Maureen stood completely still with her back to us at the counter. When she turned around, her eyes were red and bloodshot.

"Must we be so loud?" she asked.

"It was an accident," JJ said.

"I know, sweetie. I wasn't talking about you dropping the cup. I was talking about the sound the milk drops make hitting the floor." She popped two aspirin in her mouth and swallowed them without water. I wondered how a person could do that. "Don't mind me, JJ. I just seem to have picked up a little ol' bug of some sort."

It looked like the same kind of "bug" that Jack Henry used to get when he was out drinking the night before.

I'd woken up, still on the couch, when Aunt Maureen came staggering in the door with Mama helping her up the stairs. Pastor Harold slipped outside without saying a word to either one of them.

"Mm-hm." Mama winked at Aunt Maureen. "And maybe you wouldn't have picked up that 'bug' if you'd been the designated driver."

"No, no, you made the perfect one. Last night was worth it. If these blasted kids of yours would just stop making all that racket by breathing." Then she looked at me out of the corner of her eye and gave me that perfect Aunt Maureen smile. The one that lets you know that, no matter what her words say, she loves you to pieces.

Mama went to the refrigerator to get more milk. "Maureen, your stew must have been a huge hit."

"It was!" I said. Aunt Maureen flinched, so I said in a quieter voice, "Pastor Harold loved it."

"Too bad I didn't get to taste it," Mama said. "You'll have to make it again sometime."

"You can eat the leftovers, Mama," I said.

"There aren't any, sweetheart. That's why I said it must have been a hit."

"Sure there are." I got up and opened the refrigerator door. She was right. The bowl was gone.

"But . . . that doesn't make sense. I put them in here myself."

I turned and saw JJ and Caleb looking at each other. Caleb tore his eyes from JJ and said, "I got hungry in the night, ma'am."

"Oh! Well, that's just fine. Our home is yours, Caleb. If you get hungry then you can eat anything we have."

But I saw the way he had looked at JJ and I didn't believe him. Not one bit.

The doorbell rang and Aunt Maureen groaned at the sound. I ran to the door thinking it would be Pastor Harold with the load of corn he'd promised. Instead I opened the door to the biggest bouquet of flowers I'd ever seen. It was made of every color you could imagine and the scent of them made it feel like spring had paid us a visit.

I took them from the delivery boy, staggering a little under the weight, and thanked him. Then I carried them into the kitchen.

"Would you look at this!" I said.

"Oh my goodness!" Mama said, and cleared a place on the table. She grabbed the card from the bouquet and then a funny look came over her face.

"Maureen, they're for you."

"Me?" Aunt Maureen said. "Oh, Sonny needs to give up. I'm not moving back."

"They aren't from Sonny," Mama said.

Aunt Maureen frowned. "Give me that card." Then her face lit up and she cackled. She set the card on the table and leaned in to smell the flowers.

I grabbed the card before anyone could stop me. I read, "To the beautiful lady who stole my heart. Yours anytime you want, Derek."

"But you're married, Aunt Maureen," I said. "You can't be stealing anybody's heart."

"First off, sweetie, I didn't steal anybody's anything. It's not my fault if he's got a *thang* for me." She pulled a flower out of the bouquet and stuck it behind her ear. "Secondly, whether or not I'm married is debatable since I no longer live with Sonny. And second of all."

"You already said second," JJ said. "Next comes third. Even *I* know that."

"And it's a good thing I have you here to keep me straight, JJ." Aunt Maureen smiled but it was more of an annoyed one than a real grin. "*Third*, Ivy, is a lesson you need to learn right now. Never slam a door on an opportunity. Derek just might be the man of my dreams."

"He didn't seem like he'd changed much since high school to me," Mama said. "Come on, Maureen, you couldn't stand him back then!"

"Touché," Aunt Maureen said. "But what's that old expression? Something about kissing a few frogs before finding Prince Charming?"

She pulled the card from my hand and stuck it back in the plastic holder, then set the bouquet on the living room coffee table.

JJ and I followed her.

"I like Uncle Sonny," JJ said. "Why can't he be your Prince Charming anymore?"

Aunt Maureen got very still. She pushed back her hair and raised her face. When she did, her eyes were shiny.

"Would you look at me?" She wiped her nose with the back of her hand. "I guess that bug is turning into a full-blown cold."

Mama left to buy groceries and Aunt Maureen went up to rest in Mama's room. The doorbell rang again.

JJ ran to the door and threw it open. "Hi, Pastor Harold!"

"Hey, JJ." He patted JJ's head. "Are you tired from all that bird catching yesterday?"

"Nope!"

The phone rang. I waited for Aunt Maureen to pick it up.

"Well, that's good. We've got corn to unload. It's a little chilly, so you're going to need a jacket. And definitely gloves."

"Aw . . ." JJ pouted.

"For blisters. You don't want those."

"Oh, okay." JJ ran to get his jacket and gloves. Pastor Harold called after him, "Yo, sport! Is your mom here?"

I heard JJ yell out, "No! She left right after the flowers came!"

"Flowers?" Pastor Harold asked. He touched a petal of one of the pink carnations as he craned his neck at an angle to read the card. I'd snooped enough in my life to know he didn't want it to look like he was reading the card, but I knew he was.

By then the phone had rung about four times so I grabbed it.

"Hey, Ivy."

"Ellen, hey!" My heart did a triple beat. "What's up?"

"I want my things back."

"Things?" I said. "What things?"

Ellen let out a lungful of air into the phone. "The clothes I bought you. I want them back."

A million questions came to mind. *Why are you doing this to me? Why don't you want me around anymore? Aren't I hurting enough?* But all I could get out was the first word. "Why?"

"Because they're mine, that's why."

And, suddenly, I was so mad I decided not to give her the satisfaction of knowing how she hurt me.

"Hey, no problem. I'll have the clothes along with everything else you've given me over there soon. Shouldn't take long. You never gave me that much." It felt satisfying to hear her gasp. "Oh, and the stuff you have of mine? Just pitch it. I haven't given you anything that I really cared about."

"Oh, give me a break, Ivy, I can't believe you're acting so—"

This time I was the one who hung up on her.

I grabbed a garbage bag from the kitchen and took the stairs two at a time. I marched into my room, wadding the clothes she'd bought me, which, really, were a pure joy to get rid of. Then I snatched up the stuffed animals she'd given me as birthday gifts. I ripped the picture of us with our hair parted in half, one side dyed blue and one red. Our hands were stretched high in the air and our mouths open from screaming. It was taken the year Jack Henry and Mama let me bring Ellen on our family trip to the amusement park in southern Ohio. The picture got blurry so I thrust it into the bag before tears dropped on it. I didn't want Ellen to know I cared. I would *not* let her know I cried.

I didn't realize I'd kept so much of her in my room until I had to clean it out. I threw her notes away instead of giving them back. I wouldn't think about how I'd kept every one. I gave the room a once-over and saw Daisy Dog on my nightstand. I picked her up. She looked at me so friendly with her painted-on eyes and smile. I pushed her ear and she licked my finger. I sat her back by my bed. It would be the only thing I'd keep.

I threw the bag over my shoulder and headed downstairs to return it. I walked outside and saw JJ and Caleb squatted beside a bucket under a weird-shaped wagon that was hitched to the truck. Pastor Harold turned a crank and corn came out of the bottom to fill the bucket.

"Tell Mama and Aunt Maureen I'll be right back," I said.

Pastor Harold never missed a beat. He just kept turning that handle and said, "JJ will have to tell them, Ivy. I'm leaving soon. I have more important things to do."

154

He didn't look up. I tried not to let the words hurt. I was sure he did have more important things to do. Still, I had to swallow the lump in my throat.

At that minute I just wanted to strike out at somebody. I wanted to annoy Ellen and I saw the perfect way.

"On second thought, I'm pretty busy, too. Caleb, can you do something for me? I need to return these things. It's not far if you cut through the backyard to the alley, then go two blocks south. It's a yellow house. Just ring the doorbell. Tell whoever answers that this bag is from Ivy."

Caleb pushed his glasses back up on his nose and stood, deep in thought. Finally he set the bucket down and held out his hand for the bag. Then he looked at me.

I almost had second thoughts. I knew that what I was doing was mean. I remembered how Ellen had treated him in the cafeteria. But then, that's exactly why sending him to Ellen's was so perfect. She couldn't stand him. She'd hate having him there. And Caleb always did whatever anyone asked of him without arguing. I think that if he had stood up for himself, just this once, I wouldn't have insisted that he go. But, no. He just held out his hand to take the bag.

So I let him.

15

I wondered what happened when Caleb rang Ellen's doorbell but I was too proud to ask, and he didn't say one blessed word about it. When he returned, he said that he would go make sure the mess from the corn was cleaned up. Boys are dumb, if you ask me. They never feel the need to tell you the stuff you care about.

Later that evening, I was helping Mama in the kitchen. I put an onion on the chopping block and hacked.

"Isn't it nice and warm?" Mama interrupted my thoughts. "I really think I'm going to like this corn stove. I hadn't given a thought to heating this drafty place until Pastor Harold brought it up."

She stopped stirring the gravy long enough to push the hair back from her forehead. "I wish he'd taken me up on the invitation to supper, though. He practically bolted out of here when I got home. Did you notice that?"

I shrugged. "Not really."

"He's probably a very busy man," Mama said.

I shrugged again.

"What's the matter, Ivy?" she asked. Before I could answer, Aunt Maureen blew into the kitchen.

"Guess where we're going next Saturday night," she said.

"Oh, Maureen . . . you didn't," Mama said.

"Didn't what?" I asked.

Aunt Maureen slid her lanky body into a kitchen chair and said, "Sweetie, I'll give you a dollar if you'll go check to see if my clothes are dry. Five dollars if you fold them for me."

Well, I knew what was up. I knew she just wanted me out of the room so she could talk to Mama alone. Still, I didn't have any money so I asked, "Is the five dollars for folding in addition to the one dollar for checking?"

Aunt Maureen gave me that lopsided smile of hers. "You drive a hard bargain, sugar. Six dollars it is, if you go do it right now."

"Go on," Mama said. "Your aunt can finish that onion."

I walked until I was out of the kitchen, then ran to the laundry room. I opened the dryer, dumped all the clothes into a basket, and sneaked back toward the kitchen. I set the basket on the floor outside the kitchen door and gently lifted out a shirt and folded it as I listened. This was a *whole* lot better than listening to just Mama's side of the phone conversations like before.

"I said yes, Cass. I'm going out with Derek again, and I might add, that boy is just *wild* about me. And his friend

157

is taking out . . ." I didn't hear anything, so I peeked around the corner. She circled in the air with her pointer finger, then stopped when it was pointed straight at Mama. "You."

Mama shook her head as she stirred the gravy. I pulled back into the shadows so they wouldn't see me.

"Maureen, you didn't tell me you'd invited them to dinner last week. We knew Derek from school but I'm not going out with his friend."

"You've already been out with him."

"No, that's not how I see it at all. He sat at the table we did. That's all. I am not dating him. And you! You're not even legally separated from Sonny."

"Au contraire. I'd say that, considering Sonny is in Georgia and I'm in Indiana, that's about as separate as you can get."

"You know what I mean," Mama said. "You're still married."

"Yes, and I was still married when Sonny left me for weeks on end for his stupid job."

"Maureen, I know you. I know you're just hurting. If you give yourself some time, you'll see that you're still in love with Sonny. I think you're in pain now and dating Derek is salve for the wound. You need to really think about this. I'm afraid you'll get hurt."

"Hurt more than I am now? Hurt more than I am that Sonny won't even try to find another job so he's around more? And what about you? You *are* divorced, Cass. You should be having the time of your life right now. When I came here, I thought it would be like the old days, you and me partying and having fun. I've sat around doing nothing for so long. Here you are, single and pretty. We should be tearing up dance floors."

I could hear them moving around, pots clanging, spoons clinking against dishes. Then Aunt Maureen said, "Cass, remember? You were all broken up about your divorce from Travis."

Travis, if you'll remember, was my real dad's name. I stopped folding and angled for a glimpse into the kitchen so I could see them. Mama had that pained look she always got when she heard Travis's name. I learned a long time ago not to ask questions about him.

"And I took you out for a night on the town," Aunt Maureen continued.

"Maureen, don't."

She went on like she hadn't heard. "We went to hear that new band that everyone was raving about. And the lead singer? You took one look at him, Cass, and you were lost."

Mama straightened from the stove. "I was young and vulnerable."

Aunt Maureen laughed that deep laugh. "You were lost, right then and there. You took one look at Jack Henry's long dark hair hanging over his smoky blue eyes and you were a puddle. Cass, you were so much in love that you absolutely glowed. Don't you want to feel that kind of excitement again?"

"Look where it got me, Maureen. Instead of being a divorced, single mother of one child, now I've got two divorces behind me and I'm a single mother of two. I have a job and the burden of this big house to keep up. The last thing I need is for some player to bring 'excitement' into my life."

"What do you have against excitement?" Aunt Maureen asked.

"Forest fires are exciting, too, Maureen. But all they do is burn down trees."

Then they both were quiet. I picked up the laundry basket and took it to Mama's room to finish folding. I thought about what Aunt Maureen had said. I remembered how Mama was when she was with Jack Henry. She loved cooking for him and taking care of the house. It sure didn't seem to be a burden to her back then. I remembered the time Jack Henry forgot Mama's birthday and she cried. The very next night, I heard sounds downstairs and tiptoed to the staircase. There I saw a birthday cake with candles lit and Mama and Jack Henry were dancing while he sang to her. Mama sure "glowed" that night, all right.

"There she is," JJ said as he came into the room, Caleb trailing along behind. "Hey, Ivy! We were looking for you. Whatcha doin'?"

"Fishing." I sighed. "I'm folding clothes, what does it look like I'm doing?"

"Yeah, you're fishing!" He picked up a sock and shook it to look like a wiggling fish. Caleb smiled at him, then JJ dropped the sock and rolled on the bed, laughing at himself.

"Stop it, JJ!" I said. "Why don't you help me?"

"'Cause it's more fun to do this." He jumped into the middle of the stack of folded laundry.

"JJ!" I yelled. "That is *not* funny!"

He looked crestfallen. "I was trying to make you smile. You act so sad, Ivy. Just like Mama. Why is everybody always so sad around here?"

"I am not sad!" I restacked Aunt Maureen's clothes. Caleb reached to help and I gave him a look that would wilt lettuce. "And Mama's not sad."

"Uh-huh!" JJ said. "I heard her cry at night."

I stopped messing with the clothes and sat down, all thoughts of Caleb gone. JJ's room was beside Mama's. Mine was down the hall. "You did? When?"

"After Daddy left."

"But not since Aunt Maureen came, right? I mean, you don't hear her cry now, do you?"

"No, Aunt Maureen makes her laugh, but you've looked sad since Aunt Maureen came."

I didn't know what to say to that when suddenly JJ cried out, "If Daddy would just come back, everybody would be happy again!" He pushed over the stack of clothes one more time before running out of the room.

"Where did that come from?" I must have said the words, although I really was just thinking to myself.

"He's young. He doesn't remember much about his father. He thinks life was perfect as long as his dad was here so he blames anything upsetting or different on that."

"He told you that?" I asked.

"I listen." Caleb shrugged. "Sometimes it's in the things he says, sometimes it's what he does."

"Yeah, well, you didn't come here until after Mama was divorced. I mean, sure, some things were nicer before. Mama didn't have to work and there was more money. But Jack Henry didn't pay much attention to JJ or me. And he only paid attention to Mama when it was convenient. It's crazy if JJ thinks life was perfect then."

"It's normal. JJ is young enough to believe in magic. If he believes one rabbit delivers baskets to all children Easter morning, then he could believe in anything he wants, true or not," Caleb said. "Everyone wants something."

I'd never thought about it like that. I started to say that very thing to Caleb but he looked so sad. Instead I asked, "What do you want, Caleb?"

At first he didn't answer. Then, in a voice so low I could barely hear it, he said, "My parents."

16

I went to school on Monday determined to ignore Ellen. I sat with Lindsay on the bus, and as soon as I could get a word in edgewise, I asked her to eat lunch with me. I wanted to stay busy at lunch so I wouldn't be staring at Alexa's table.

"We sat at the same table all last week," she said. "Why the special invitation?"

"Oh! No reason." Had I really been so tuned in to what Ellen was doing that I didn't even realize Lindsay was there all along? It made me feel bad, so I paid extra attention to Lindsay on the ride to school.

And I did do a better job of ignoring Ellen, so much that it wasn't until lunch that I noticed she wasn't sitting with Alexa's group.

"Have you seen Ellen?" I asked Lindsay.

"She didn't come today." Lindsay frowned. "I told you that when we sat down. Weren't you listening?"

So much for thinking I was doing a great job of

ignoring Ellen. Instead, I'd ignored Lindsay. To make up for it, I said, "I was wondering if you'd like to go to the next football game with me."

"Sure!" she said.

That afternoon, when we reached our bus stop, Lindsay stood to let me leave. "So, we're on for the football game, right?"

"Right. Sounds good!" I called on my way out, and realized that I really meant it.

JJ ran into the house first, straight for the kitchen. Aunt Maureen peeled the paper off an ice cream sandwich and handed it to JJ. He ran outside just as the phone rang.

"Oh! Good, I've been waiting on that pastor to call all day." She punched the phone.

"Hello? Sonny! I wasn't expecting you." Her voice dropped. "Please don't do this to me. You want me to come back but it would be to an empty house. You say you'll look for another job but you've said that before. The next thing I know, you'll be back on the road."

She made me feel sorry for Uncle Sonny. I should have given her privacy but I also wanted to hear what she said, so I quietly opened an ice cream sandwich for myself and listened.

"Sonny, you've got to get over me." Aunt Maureen dabbed at her eyes. I knew she was crying but I'll bet Uncle Sonny didn't because her voice didn't show it.

"There's something you should know. I have a date Saturday night."

I couldn't hear what Uncle Sonny said, but whatever it was, it wasn't enough to make Aunt Maureen go back home.

"Please stop. I love you but we don't work anymore. I have to go now. Goodbye."

She had just clicked off when the phone rang again.

"I just can't take any more." She took a deep breath, then looked at the caller ID. "Oh, thank goodness. It's not Sonny. It's the pastor."

She said hello and walked down the hall. I couldn't imagine what she wanted Pastor Harold for so I was glad when she came back into the room, still talking.

"Well, you seemed eager enough to help Cass out earlier, without her even asking, I might add."

She listened and said, "Uh-huh. Uh-huh. Well, you just go on about your business then and don't worry that a member of your flock needs your help."

She shut the phone off and muttered, "That man!"

"What is it?" I asked. Mama would have shooed me away but Aunt Maureen didn't seem to worry about hiding things the way Mama did.

"I told that preacher your mama and I have dates Saturday night and asked him to sit for you guys again."

I glared at her as she said, "I promised your mama I'd find someone and every single person on her list of sitters is busy that night. I thought that preacher would come over, but no, he has *plans*. I guess I'll just have to keep looking."

And there she went again, acting like JJ was her responsibility, not mine.

"JJ is my brother," I said. "I took care of him before you came. You shouldn't be asking people to take care of him. It's my job!"

She folded her arms and leaned back.

"So, Miss Ivy, it would appear I've stepped on your toes somehow."

"Just because you happened to call one night when things were a little crazy around here doesn't mean I wanted you to take over," I said. "I never asked you to come!"

She picked lint off her sweater, like my words hadn't bothered her one tiny bit, but I could see the hurt in her eyes. Trouble was, I was plenty hurt myself.

"Well, I guess I wasn't asked, at that," she said.

She got up and put the dishes in the sink. "You know what, Ivy? Today hasn't been easy. I think I'll get a manicure and try to relax and you can have that time with JJ that you want. Be sure and have dinner ready by the time your mama gets home, okay?"

Then she grabbed her purse and left. I hadn't counted on having to cook but maybe Mama would bring home some food. If not, I'd find something. I could take care of my family. I wanted to and Aunt Maureen could just go on her dates, get manicures, and whatever else she wanted to do. That was just fine with me.

★ ★ ★

I woke up on Saturday morning to the sound of the phone ringing and then Mama scurrying around. I didn't have to go too far down the hall to hear her tell Aunt Maureen, "I'll do the best I can but Magdalena gave me a job when no one else would. If she's shorthanded and needs me today, then I have no choice."

"Are you sure you didn't cook this up to try to get out of our dates tonight?" Aunt Maureen asked.

"*Your* date, Maureen. I'm just going along to keep you from doing anything foolish."

"Derek is bringing along his friend for you!" Aunt Maureen called through the bathroom door after Mama closed it.

"That's his problem!" Mama shouted back.

"Don't mess this up for me, Cass," Aunt Maureen said in a stern voice. Then it softened. "Please."

The bathroom door flew open and Mama buttoned the top button of her blouse as she hurried down the stairs with Aunt Maureen on her tail.

"I said I'd go, so I'll go. I just might be running a little late. You did find a sitter, right? Because I won't go that far away from my children without one."

"Yes, I did. The manicurist recommended a girl that she uses and she was available."

"What's her name?"

"Jada Wilson. She's a freshman and her parents are dentists."

It was bad enough having Aunt Maureen taking over

with JJ. I wasn't going to sit there and have some girl not much older than me watching *my* brother. It was time I took charge again. I didn't know Jada but it wasn't hard finding her number. The phone book listed Drs. Wilson and Wilson under dentists, with their residence beneath their office. I wrote it down and stuffed the slip of paper into my pocket to use when it was almost time for Mama and Aunt Maureen to leave. By then it would be too late for them to do anything about it.

Later that day, when Aunt Maureen was trying on dresses and it was almost time for Mama to come home, I grabbed the phone from the hall, took it into my room, and closed the door. I pulled out the number and dialed.

"Hello?"

Putting on my best "mother" voice, I said, "May I speak to Jada?"

"Jada is in the shower. This is her mother. Would you like me to have her call you?"

"No," I said. "This is Cass Henry. I'm afraid we won't need Jada to babysit tonight after all. Our plans have changed. We've heard good things about her, though. We'll call again soon."

I said my goodbyes and then called Lindsay.

"Hey!" she said. "Want to hang out?"

"Well, not right now but I need a favor. I can call out on our phone but I'm not sure people are able to call in. Will you hang up and try to call me?"

"Sure!" she said. We hung up. A moment later the phone rang. I made sure I picked it up before anyone else could.

"I guess it's working now. Thanks, Lindsay!"

"Sure! Too bad you can't hang out. I'll bet my mom would take us to a movie."

I hesitated for a minute. I mean, not that I could go to a movie tonight, even if I wanted to. But I wondered: when was the last time Ellen sounded so happy to hear from me?

"I can't, Lindsay," I said. "But I truly wish I could." And that's the funny part. I really did.

I said goodbye and then remembered why I'd called her in the first place. "Aunt Maureen? That call was from Jada Wilson," I lied. "She said she'd be a little late tonight but not to worry."

Aunt Maureen stepped out of Mama's bedroom where she was getting ready. "Did she say how long she'd be?"

"No, just that you shouldn't hold up your plans. She promised she'd only be a few minutes late."

I turned to go back into my room and saw JJ, his head tilted, looking at me funny. I felt a twinge of guilt. Did he know what I'd just done? I shrugged it off. How could he? I hopped on my bed, scooted Aunt Maureen's iPod Shuffle aside, and popped my favorite CD in my old player, feeling good about being back in charge.

Mama got home "just in the nick of time" according

to Aunt Maureen, who whisked her into the bathroom, where she already had the shower running.

I warmed up the fried chicken, mashed potatoes, and peas that Mama brought from Dining Divinely.

"Peas? Blech! I'd rather eat mud cookies!" JJ said.

"Mud cookies?!" I said.

"Caleb told me about them. People in Haiti eat mud!"

I took a deep breath and counted to ten. I'd won JJ back from Aunt Maureen but I still had Caleb to deal with. To get his mind on something else, I said, "We're going to have fun tonight, JJ. Maybe we'll watch a movie together and eat popcorn."

"Where are Mama and Aunt Maureen going?"

"Out dancing, I guess," I said.

"Because it's Saturday night, right?" He bit into a chicken leg. "People always go to music places on Saturday night!"

"Well, not all people," I said.

"But some do. Mama is. It's a musical night! Right, Caleb?"

Caleb smiled. "I suppose any night could be a musical one."

"But Saturday night is when Daddy used to be gone all night playing. It's the best musical night." He hopped from his chair, wiped his mouth, and ran off to play.

I had just finished washing the silverware and Caleb was gathering the garbage when Mama and Aunt Maureen came downstairs. Mama looked just as pretty as the last time, but she didn't look at all happy about going.

She walked over to me and put one hand on each side of my face. "Sugar, are you positive you're going to be all right until the babysitter gets here? Maybe we should wait until then."

"Mama! You're treating me like a baby. She said she'd be here soon and lots of girls my age babysit. We'll be fine."

She sighed. "I guess you're right. I gave JJ a kiss and told him to be good. I wish I had a cell phone. Call Aunt Maureen's if you need anything."

"I will."

She told Caleb goodbye, then they were gone.

17

The phone rang and I hurried to answer, thinking that Mama might have forgotten something. Was I ever surprised when I heard Ellen's voice!

"Ivy!" She sounded upset. "Ivy, I asked you to bring me the things I bought you. I need them back now!"

"I . . . I already did!"

"No, you didn't, and now I'm in so much trouble." She hiccuped because she was crying so hard.

"Ellen, calm down. What's wrong?"

"Only . . . the end . . . of the . . . world." She hiccuped between every few words.

"I'll come right over," I said.

"No! I'm not at home!" she practically yelled. "And if my mother calls, you don't know where I am! Bring the stuff to the mall. I'll wait for you by Catie's Closet."

"But I don't have your stuff! I sent it to you with Caleb last Saturday. Didn't you get it?"

"Caleb?" she said. "Oh, no! Ivy, you didn't!"

"What?"

"When I saw that lowlife, Caleb, I told him to get off our property. He dropped a bag and I threw it in the trash can by the curb! Oh, Ivy, don't tell me it had those clothes in it!"

Now, I'll admit that, to annoy Ellen, I sent Caleb instead of delivering the bag myself. I'll take the blame for that. But I never in a million years thought he'd get treated so badly by her.

"Well, it serves you right, doesn't it, Ellen? I mean, Caleb delivered them because I asked him to! And he was just bringing back the *junky* stuff you gave me, anyway. What's the big deal?" I was breathing hard because I was so mad, but there was only silence on her end. When she finally answered, she was flat-out sobbing.

"The big deal is that I took my mom's credit card out of her purse to buy it. And now, if I can't get a refund from the store, then my mom will know what happened."

"But I wore them! How could you have gotten a refund, anyway?"

"You'd only worn them once, Ivy. It might have worked."

"Oh, Ellen! Why would you do such a dumb thing?"

"Because Alexa uses her mom's card all the time. So when she bought stuff for herself, I bought some for me. I even threw in those things for you. Alexa told me that if Mom noticed, she would think it was identity theft and the credit card company wouldn't make her pay!

173

But that's not good enough for *my* mom. I heard her tell them she wanted the store to look at their surveillance cameras!"

Time sort of slowed down. It had to because too many thoughts ran through my brain for it to be working on regular time. I wondered what happened to the Ellen I'd always known. She never broke rules, not even when we were little. And what would happen to her? I shuddered, thinking what it would be like if it were me and my mama found out that I'd stolen her credit card. I felt bad that Ellen bought me the stuff in the first place, but then I remembered how she'd practically forced it on me. Truth be told, Ellen had only bought me those clothes so I'd look "cool" to Alexa's friends at her stupid party. And I guess that thought made me catch up to real time.

"Ellen, I don't know what I can do."

"Yeah, well, thanks for nothing!" she said, and hung up.

I knew I should leave well enough alone. I hadn't brought any of this on. But Ellen sounded so torn up and a part of me felt guilty for not taking the stuff to her myself. If I had, Caleb wouldn't have been made to feel bad, and surely he had. Plus Ellen wouldn't be in this mess. So I ran out the door, thinking I'd get to Catie's Closet and somehow try to help her.

"Guys! I'll be right back!" I shouted loud enough for Caleb and JJ to hear.

I knew I'd get there faster if I rode so I went to the garage and found my bicycle. I got on it and headed out.

I pumped my legs harder than I ever had and finally got to the mall, but Ellen wasn't in front of Catie's Closet. I went inside and didn't find her there, either.

"Excuse me," I asked the saleswoman. "Was there a girl about my age here?"

"Honey, there've been girls about your age in here all day long. Can you be more specific?"

"Real skinny. Brown hair. So tall." I raised my hand to just below my height.

The woman let out a loud sigh. "That pretty much describes everyone I've seen today. I don't know if your friend is here. I suggest you look around. Sorry I can't be more help."

I checked in the dressing rooms and then went outside. She still wasn't there so I waited a while. I wished I'd brought a jacket because it was getting cool. The sky was darker than it should be for this time of day, too. I finally decided I'd better hurry back in case it rained.

I pedaled toward home and was almost there when the first fat drop of rain hit the top of my head. Then more came down and splattered my back. Lightning streaked across the sky as I threw down my bike and ran to our porch. I looked back and saw fierce-looking clouds rolling in.

"Caleb? JJ?" I called as I flipped the light switch. "Where are you guys?"

There was no answer.

A crack of lightning sent a flash through the room.

Storms didn't usually bother me but there was something eerie about this one. Maybe it was because Mama wasn't in town. I didn't want to be alone and I sure as heck didn't want JJ to be.

"JJ! Answer me!" I ran to his room but he wasn't there. I yanked open his closet door but he wasn't in there, either. Next I looked in the bathroom, but no JJ. Beads of sweat popped out on my forehead.

Where could they have gone? I swallowed hard, trying to keep down the fear that something might have happened to my brother. I shouldn't have left him with Caleb. Hadn't I said all along we didn't know him well enough? I went back into JJ's room and yanked the covers off his unmade bed, then looked underneath. I found an assortment of toys and dust. There was a worn-out stuffed puppy he'd dragged around with him when he was a little guy. I sniffed it and it smelled just like he used to, sort of a mixture of peanut butter, Kool-Aid, and sleep.

Tears filled my eyes. I had to sit down for a minute. I lowered myself onto his beanbag chair and felt a sharp pain in my hip.

"Ow!" I reached under my bottom and realized I'd sat on JJ's small but real guitar that Jack Henry had bought him. I remembered the times he'd sit with JJ on his lap, showing him chords. JJ had begged Jack Henry to take him to Harmony Street Blues, but Jack Henry always said, "Some Saturday night we'll do that." Of course, that Saturday night never came.

But this was Saturday night.

Would JJ and Caleb have gone there? No. But after thinking and thinking, it was the only idea that I could come up with. Besides, if going there didn't help me find JJ, maybe it might lead to a better idea. Looking anywhere was better than sitting here alone.

Like a rocket, I shot out of that beanbag chair and ran down the stairs and out the front door.

Thunder clapped so loud it felt like the sky had broken apart and was about to cave in on me, but I didn't slow down. If JJ was out in this he was scared, and that meant he needed me.

I hurried down the street. The wet puddles soaked my sneakers and a pain started in my side, but I gritted my teeth and ignored it. I ran all the harder when I heard music coming from Harmony Street Blues.

I looked in the glass front door. It was too dark inside to see so I rapped on the window and called "JJ!"

The door swung open and a man said, "You're too young to come inside, miss."

"I'm looking for my brother. He's only five."

The man chuckled. "If you're too young, do you think we'd let a five-year-old inside? Go on home, now."

He closed the door. The wind, mixed with rain, tore at my clothes and slapped my face. Splashes of rain rolled off me. Or maybe they were tears. At that point I didn't know. I just knew I'd lost JJ and had no idea where he was.

I felt something warm touch me. I jumped, spun around, and screamed. A man was holding out a plastic bag to me, just like the one he wore as a rain cover. I began backing up when Caleb came from behind the man, sidestepped him, and put his hand on my arm.

The man backed into the shadows. I held on to Caleb, never so happy to see anyone, even him, in my entire life.

I rubbed the spot where the man had touched me as if he'd branded me with an iron.

Caleb said something but I couldn't make it out. "What?" I leaned in closer.

"Don't be afraid. He was just trying to give you something to cover up with." Then, his next words penetrated. The whistling wind died and the flashes of lightning ceased to matter to me. I felt as if the clouds had parted and the sun had broken through when he said, "Come on. I know where JJ is."

I followed Caleb to the alley behind Harmony Street Blues. By now the rain was coming down hard and it was difficult to see, so I just kept my eyes on Caleb's back and trusted him. He ran to the Dumpsters lined up against a building, threw open the doors, and peered inside each until he came to the third one. His movements slowed and I could hear him murmuring into the bin.

I moved closer and saw brown hair. It was JJ. My God above! I almost slid to the wet ground in relief. Instead I opened the lid to the Dumpster wider. JJ looked up at me, blinking as the rain pelted his little face. I quickly lowered the lid as Caleb had done so that it provided him some shelter.

Caleb pulled on my arm to get my attention, then cradled his hands together and stooped so that I could use his hand to climb inside.

"I don't understand," I yelled over the rain.

"Until the storm passes," he said. I didn't give the smell of the empty Dumpster any thought at all as I put my foot on his hands and climbed in with JJ. Next Caleb slid in beside us and lowered the door.

I hugged JJ and rocked him.

"Ivy, are you scared, too?" he asked.

"I was." I pulled back to look at him. "I couldn't find you, JJ."

"I wasn't lost," he said. "I knew exactly where I was. I'm not in trouble, am I?"

"No," I said. I mean, really, how could I have been mad when I thought he was lost and I might never see him again? It would all have been my fault, too. But I was a little angry at Caleb.

"Weren't you watching JJ?" I asked him.

"Don't yell at Caleb, Ivy!" JJ said. "I know you didn't want a babysitter today. I know you told Aunt Maureen a fib so we wouldn't have one. So I did the same thing. I told Caleb I was going to take a nap. I hid in my room and then sneaked out when he was busy. I did it because I didn't want a babysitter, either!"

If I'd ever wondered where the exact location of my heart was—you know, center of my chest? left of center?—I knew at that moment, because there was a pain so sharp in it I thought I'd die from the hurt.

I'd been mad at every single person I knew for lying, Caleb most of all, but it was me that had caused the most pain. I'd almost lost JJ because he heard my lie.

"I'm really sorry," I said in a small voice. I looked at Caleb and repeated it. "I'm so sorry."

Caleb shook his head and took off his glasses to wipe the rain from them. "I should have known. JJ and I sometimes came here together to look for his father. I thought his dad might actually be here and I knew how much JJ wanted to see him."

"What?" I said. "You *knew* he was coming here and you didn't stop him? You didn't tell anyone?"

Caleb hung his head. "It seemed like an innocent thing to do. I was always with him."

"But not tonight, Caleb. What about tonight?"

"I thought he was napping. Then I realized he was gone and you weren't home to tell."

I felt a pang at that, but kept on. "Still, you should have let someone know!"

"Maybe I should have left a note."

"Gee, do you think?" I said with as much sarcasm as I could.

"But it was raining and all I could think about was getting to him."

The same thing I had thought. I hadn't left a note for him when I went searching for JJ. It seemed like everything came back to how I'd messed up tonight.

I looked down at JJ. His face was puckered and he looked just miserable.

"Daddy didn't come, Ivy," he said. "It's Saturday night. Music night. But he's not here and I don't think he's ever gonna come back." His whole body began to shake and he buried his face into my neck, throwing his little arms around me as he cried.

18

Caleb carried JJ home. The rain had slowed to a fine mist and I was grateful to see a few lights on in the house. I opened the door for Caleb and then ran upstairs and poured JJ's bathwater. JJ was so tired that he barely stayed awake while I washed him. Together, Caleb and I got him to bed. I kissed him and then left Caleb to say good night.

As I walked by Caleb's room, I glanced in and saw a binder on the floor. It looked so out of place. I mean, if there was one thing you could count on, it was that Caleb's room was the cleanest in the house. I stepped inside and picked it up. I intended to put it back on his makeshift bookcase, truly. But then I realized it had clear sleeves that held handwritten letters. The page it was open to had the words "mud cookies" underlined and an exclamation point. Well, I ask you, would you have been able not to read it when JJ had just talked about them?

I sat down and read the pretty cursive.

"There is so much hunger here. To ease the emptiness in their stomachs, the Haitians eat <u>mud cookies</u>! They actually take mud and sift the rocks and clumps from it, then mix in salt and shortening. They flatten the mud into round shapes and spread them out on rooftops for the sun to bake. It breaks my heart to see them eating these just to have something in their stomachs. I often take them my food instead."

I felt the bed shift as Caleb sat next to me, hands in his lap, head down.

"JJ mentioned mud cookies at supper. You've told him this story."

Caleb nodded.

"And the man in the alley, JJ knows him?" The pieces started falling into place. "Has he been taking our food to this person?"

"He told me that he'd been trying to find his dad at the place where he used to play music. He took me there and said sometimes there are . . . he called them Haitians but he had to have confused the Haitians in the stories with homeless people. Like the one who offered you the plastic bag. He said he took them food from home so they won't eat mud cookies. Once I knew, I made him promise to never go alone. I said I wouldn't tell as long as I could come to keep him safe."

I had no answer to that. I thought of JJ, brave enough to take food to people he didn't know.

"He could have been in danger."

"That's why I followed. To watch after him."

Then I looked back at the binder.

"This isn't your handwriting," I said.

Caleb looked at me and shook his head but he didn't yank the book out of my hands or tell me to put it down. I turned the page. There were more letters. Some were in a man's handwriting and were signed "Dad." The fancier handwriting was signed "Mom." What didn't add up was how loving these letters were when I knew Caleb's parents hadn't called or written the whole time he'd been here.

In the letters I recognized bits of the stories Caleb had been telling JJ. I read about how his dad took a shower with someone peeping in. I read about riding in a tap tap.

He handed me another book and it was the journal his mother kept in Haiti. Some of the stories I hadn't heard, but I recognized the one where his parents let a boy bring his mattress into their tent on rainy nights.

I picked up a small scrapbook. It had newspaper clippings. The headlines said, "Haiti Devastated by Massive Earthquake," "2010 Earthquake Worst in Haiti for 200 Years," and "Local Citizens Confirmed Dead in Earthquake." There were two photos on the page. The man looked thinner and younger than Caleb's dad. The woman was very pretty and younger than the one who had come to our house. In fact, she didn't look anything like her. In the picture, this lady had kind eyes and a big smile. Below their pictures were their obituaries. I read how they were missionaries working in Haiti. At the bottom I read, "They are survived by their son, Caleb."

I looked at him. He hadn't moved.

"Caleb." My voice surprised me. It sounded so thick. "This is your mom and dad, right?"

That's when he raised his eyes to mine and I noticed how much they looked like the eyes of the woman in the picture—his mom.

He said, "The witch doctors in Haiti take poison from puffer fish and give it to humans." My brain registered he wasn't directly answering my question, but this time I knew that—if I really listened to Caleb's stories—he'd give me an answer.

"The poison made their breathing and heartbeat slow almost to a complete stop," he said. "People would think that person had died, and they buried them. Then the witch doctor would use 'voodoo' to bring them back to life. It made people think the witch doctors were very powerful. Of course, the people were never really dead to begin with. But they were called the living dead."

Caleb took the book from my hands and looked at the picture of his parents. "These letters are all I have. And the stories of Haiti that my parents told me. When I miss them, I just have to open these books and here they are, written down for me to remember."

He closed the scrapbook and put it on the shelf. "It's easier to think that my parents are really waiting on a witch doctor to bring them back to life. It's easier for me to talk about Haiti than it is to talk about anything else. It's all I have of them."

"But what about the people who brought you here? If they aren't your parents, who are they?"

"My parents' only living relatives are my father's cousin and his wife. I stayed with them when my parents did their mission work."

"I knew it!" I said. "I *knew* they weren't real missionaries!"

"There are different kinds of missionaries. My parents traveled to Haiti. They do work here."

"But I thought missionaries were good people who helped others. What kind of people are they if they don't take care of you?"

"They aren't bad people. They just didn't plan on raising another child. My parents only meant for me to stay with them for a short while." He sighed. "They were to come back for me in a few months."

Bang! Bang!

Caleb and I both jumped. He bolted for the stairs. I was fast on his tail.

As soon as I hit the bottom step, I saw Pastor Harold beating on the door, then cupping his hands around his eyes, looking in the front door window. I hurried to open it.

"Are you two okay?" he asked. "Where's JJ?"

"JJ's asleep. We're fine," I told him. He looked like he'd been caught in a hurricane. "What happened to you?"

"My phone went out. I thought you guys might be here alone so I started over and drove through a flash flood. My motor died." He stepped inside and peeled off his wet jacket. "Think you could get me a towel?"

Caleb got one while I hung his jacket over the back of a chair.

"The storm came up so quickly!" he said. "I couldn't get here fast enough to check on you guys and then my stupid car died. Thank God the worst of it missed us and you three were home safe."

Caleb and I looked at each other. He didn't say anything but I did. "JJ ran off tonight. Something happened to my friend and I left to help her. I don't know what I was thinking, leaving like that. When I came back, he wasn't here."

"It's my fault, too," Caleb said. "But together we found him and he's safe now."

I looked at Caleb and remembered him saving me with the bird's nest after Alexa's party. Here he was helping me again. It seemed to me that Caleb was behaving like the friend I wanted Ellen to be—and that Ellen wasn't.

I wrapped my arms around myself and sat down. Suddenly the bad weather and the scare with JJ made me so cold I started shaking. Pastor Harold noticed.

"I plan to spend the night here on the couch. I think you two must have done just fine if JJ's safe. I can't blame you when I thought you were here alone and I didn't come over." He drew the afghan around my shoulders.

"You can't help it if you had plans," I said.

"That's just it. I didn't really have plans." He sighed. "It's a long story and we've had a rough night. You two get upstairs to bed and we'll talk in the morning."

But I felt so cozy in the chair, all snug in the afghan. "I think I'll rest here for a while."

And, because it was a rainy night and because I knew Caleb's parents let the boy stay in their tent, I said, "Caleb? You should bring your pillow and stay here, too."

The last thing I saw before I fell asleep was a big smile on his face.

It was pitch-black in the room when I heard the front door open. I was afraid to move. Then I remembered that Pastor Harold was there and I felt safer.

"Stop being mad at me. If the phone lines weren't down, we could have called to see how they are."

"Mama?" I said.

Mama's intake of breath sounded louder than a scream. Then Pastor Harold threw on the light just as Aunt Maureen stepped on Caleb's foot, startling him so that he yelped.

Mama and Aunt Maureen hugged each other in fright.

Pastor Harold said, "Cass! It's okay."

"What, in heaven's name, is going on here?" Mama yelled.

Well, all the commotion was enough to wake the dead, let alone JJ, who cried out, "Ivy!"

Mama and Aunt Maureen looked toward the stairs,

but when Pastor Harold again said, "Cass," Mama took a step toward him.

Aunt Maureen looked around. "Where is the babysitter? Why are you here, Harold?"

"There wasn't a babysitter," he said.

"But I called one. Ivy, where's Jada?"

"I . . ." This was going to be hard. "I told her not to come."

"Ivy Greer!" Mama said. "You kids were here alone?"

"Ivy." Aunt Maureen began crying. "Oh, baby, do you resent me that much? I never meant to take over. I just . . . well . . . I love you kids so."

And instead of yelling at me, she came and hugged me.

"I'm sorry, Aunt Maureen," I said.

I knew I'd better get the worst part over with. "And, Mama, that's not all. JJ ran off by himself tonight. But—Caleb and I—together we found him."

Mama lowered herself onto the edge of a chair. Her face was white. "My goodness. I can't believe this mess. I *never* would have left if I'd known all this was going to happen. I feel like the world's worst mother."

"They're safe now, Cass," Pastor Harold said.

JJ called my name again. Maybe it was because I was all snuggly in the afghan and chair. Maybe it was because I didn't want to miss out on what Pastor Harold and Mama talked about. But I like to think, at that moment, I realized how hard it was on Aunt Maureen not having kids of her own to look after, and that she might not have been trying to take my job away as much as trying to fill that hole in her heart.

"Aunt Maureen?" I said. "Would you please check on JJ?"

She smiled at me and was off like a shot.

"I heard there was a storm headed this way," Mama said. "We tried to call. At first we thought Maureen's cell phone had run out of minutes. Then we tried a pay phone and learned that the phones were down. It was the longest ride home from Indianapolis! But I had to know that everyone was all right."

"Everyone is fine," Pastor Harold said, only he didn't look like he was "fine." He looked downright miserable.

"Why are you here, Harold?" Mama asked.

"To check on the kids. Make sure they were okay. I'll head on home now. Sorry you had to cut your date short."

"It wasn't a *date*," Mama said. "I went along to keep Maureen out of trouble."

"Yeah, well, I saw the flowers that guy sent you. *He* must have thought it was a date."

"Flowers? Those were Maureen's." Then Mama's eyes lit up. "Harold, did you think I had an admirer?"

"A beautiful woman like you? Yes, Cass. I'm sure you have lots of them," he said.

Mama studied him for a moment. Then she went over and sat by him on the couch.

"I don't have a boyfriend, Harold. And I don't have

any admirers. At least none that will come forward and ask me on a date."

I was completely awake now, staying as still as a piece of furniture so I didn't miss one word. I slid my eyes to Caleb. He appeared to be asleep but I knew better. Like he'd told me before, Caleb listened.

"Maybe you have an admirer who knows he has very slim prospects," Pastor Harold said.

Mama took his hand. "Maybe he should tell me about those prospects."

"Oh, Cass," he said. "I have thought about you every minute since you first came to church. But I don't make much money as a pastor. And let's not forget that I'm an *interim* one at that. I already know that, in four months, I'm being moved to a church in St. Cloud. That's forty minutes away. And, even if I could stay here, I don't have the money to woo you with fancy dates or send big bouquets of flowers."

"Let me tell you a story," Mama said. "I had someone who wrote love songs about me. I had someone who swept me off my feet, and do you know where it got me? Knocked off my feet is all. Harold, you're good and steady. You think about how I'm going to heat my house. You worry about my kids being alone in a storm. Those are all pretty romantic things to me.

"I know you have to move. But that's four months from now. And, as you said, St. Cloud is only forty minutes away. You'll be there at least six months, right? That adds up to ten months. I think I'd rather spend the next ten months getting to know you better than ignoring you because of where you might move next. And as far as you not making a lot of money, well, I've learned I can live without much of that, too."

Pastor Harold's smile was brighter than the sun. "Well, then, Cass Henry, I would be honored if you would go on a date with me."

And I'm not sure, but I think they might have kissed right then and there if not for a knock on the door that startled us all.

Mama's hand flew to her chest. "I'm not sure how much more of this I can take tonight," she said.

Aunt Maureen came down the stairs holding JJ. The door swung open and there stood Uncle Sonny. Big, lovable, huggable Uncle Sonny calling out, "Maureen! It's time to come home!"

19

The next day I could hear Mama and Aunt Maureen giggling from her bedroom. I loved the sound of it. I heard Mama say, "Last night wasn't much different than junior high."

Well, I was in junior high now and I was curious and tired of listening but pretending not to. I got my courage up and knocked on Mama's partially open door.

She looked up and saw me. "Come on in, honey. We're just having a little girl-talk."

"And I'm invited?" I asked.

She laughed. "Well, sure. You're a girl, aren't you? Besides, you might appreciate this story."

Aunt Maureen said, "It's when we were about your age."

I curled up next to Aunt Maureen on the bed.

"And we were sworn enemies," Mama said.

"You two? You've been best friends for *eons*!" I said.

"True," Aunt Maureen said. "But you can't be best friends for that long and not have some humdinger fights."

"Like last night," Mama said. "I wanted to kill Maureen. She had no business being on that date."

"True," Aunt Maureen admitted.

"And I had to go along to make sure she didn't do anything stupid."

"Which was exactly what I did to your mom in junior high." She lowered her voice, like she was talking just to me. "She fell for a high school jock with a smooth line."

"My mother was so strict and I just wanted some freedom," Mama said. "Plus he was an eleven on a scale of one to ten."

"Says you," Aunt Maureen said. "And your taste in men hasn't improved much."

Mama swatted at her. "Take that back."

"Okay," Aunt Maureen said. "I've been too hard on poor Pastor Harold."

"Thank you for finally admitting it! Anyway, Maureen jumped in the backseat of the car and went with me and the high school jock on our date. He knew he wasn't going to get any kisses from me with my best friend watching so he took us home. I was so mad at Maureen that I didn't speak to her for weeks. I found new friends and planned to never talk to her again."

"You fell in with the wrong crowd," Aunt Maureen said. "Admit it. You missed me."

"Well, duh!" Mama said. "Here we are years later, still

having boy trouble, still arguing, and still being there for each other. Of course I missed you."

"But I don't understand," I said. "I thought you two were always close, no matter what."

"Oh, Ivy, honey," Aunt Maureen said. "Life is full of ups and downs. Look at me. Here I had completely given up on Sonny being there for me."

She was sure wrong about that. When Uncle Sonny came in the night before, he explained to Aunt Maureen— right in front of all of us—that he hadn't driven his big rig to see her because he had quit his job. He had hopped on an airplane with nothing but a yearning to win her back.

"I was so lonely that I was ready to walk out on a good man," she said. "Speaking of . . . I need to go give that husband of mine another kiss. Can you believe how he flew in like that? A regular knight in shining armor."

Mama laughed and they left the room. That's when I thought of Ellen. I'd like to think that someday we'd be old and laughing and telling stories about the time she fell in with the wrong crowd, but I don't think all friendships are like Mama and Aunt Maureen's. I couldn't see Ellen jumping into a car to save me from the wrong boy. And she didn't want my help in saving her from the wrong friend.

I'd called Ellen earlier that morning, begging her to tell her mom that she had stolen her credit card. "I'll even sit with you when you talk to her. It'll be like it used to be. Ellen Waite and Ivy League, against the world," I'd said. "She'll be mad at first, but if you apologize from your heart, she'll forgive you."

"Alexa said to wait it out. She said the store has *miles* of surveillance tape. They'll never find it and this will all blow over."

"But, Ellen, do you really want to steal? I mean, nothing could be worth how upset you were yesterday."

"I'm just fine, Ivy. Besides, Alexa and I have fun. We . . . well, she's more like who I want to be. I don't have to beg her to get dressed up for a party or remind her to brush her hair."

And that's when I knew that Ellen and I were probably not going to be like Mama and Aunt Maureen. But then I thought about Lindsay. I knew I would still sit with her on the bus and I'd still eat lunch with her. I knew we'd go to football games and movies together because she liked me as I was. To me, that's what makes someone a real friend.

And then there's Caleb. I had to think of him as a friend, too. I mean, who'd put up with the way I treated him and still be nice to me if he didn't want me as a friend?

Thinking about Caleb made me realize I hadn't seen him all morning. I went downstairs and saw Uncle Sonny on the front porch, his arm protectively around Aunt Maureen. They appeared to be deep in discussion with Pastor Harold and Caleb.

I opened the door and stepped out.

Caleb saw me and his face split into an ear-to-ear grin. "So that would make Ivy my cousin?"

"Your cousin!" I said.

Everyone chuckled but Uncle Sonny's booming laugh was the loudest, warming me clear through.

"What are you talking about?" I said.

"Caleb tells me that you know the Bennetts are his guardians, right?" Pastor Harold said.

"Yeah, I mean, I thought they were his mom and dad," I said. "Hey, wait a minute, Pastor Harold. You knew?"

"I admit to not knowing until you prompted me to look into the situation."

"Why didn't you tell me?" I put my hands on my hips.

"Whoa, young lady," Mama said as she joined us on the porch, carrying JJ. "Before you get too angry, it wasn't a secret. I knew. I thought you did, too."

"Well, I didn't!" I said. Then I realized why. "But I guess I never asked him, either."

"The point is, Caleb's guardians want him taken care of and provided for but it's hard at their age. They weren't expecting to raise another child."

I suddenly felt very protective of Caleb. Everyone deserved to be wanted.

"So, stay with us, Caleb," I told him. "We want you."

"Yeah, Caleb!" JJ jumped down from Mama and wrapped his arms around Caleb's waist. "You can stay here forever!"

"Actually, Pastor Harold is going to talk to the Bennetts about transferring guardianship to your uncle Sonny and me," Aunt Maureen said. "We have to meet with them, get their approval, become certified as foster parents and all. But . . ." She gazed at Caleb and she looked so soft and pretty, longing for the chance to be someone's mother. "But he'll be worth it."

And I looked at Caleb. Still tall and gangly. Still having to push his glasses up on his nose. Still a little different from anyone I knew.

"Yeah," I said. "He'll be worth it."

And that's the truth.

Acknowledgments

I have been fortunate to know the Don and Jane Marshall family of Indiana. While Jane kept the home fires burning, Don traveled as a missionary in northwest Haiti. In 1996, he took one of their daughters, Donja, then fifteen years old, with him on her first mission trip. Among the many mission trips the girls participated in, Donja made eight such ventures to Haiti and her sister, Amanda, made six journeys there. Both girls kept journals of these trips, portions of which were previously published in their local newspapers, the *Fountain County Neighbor* and the *Review Republican.*

A few of their tales worked their way into my book, such as the outdoor shower story that Caleb tells JJ, as well as the story of the boy with no poles for his tent. Thank you, Donja and Amanda, for giving me a glimpse of your time there and for sharing your stories with me (and Caleb, of course).

I would be remiss if I didn't mention John J. Bonk and Lisa Williams Kline, who, once again, provided invaluable feedback. Thanks, guys.